SEE ME, HEAR ME

SEE ME, HEAR ME

BY THE RIVERSIDE

Robin Fortier

To order additional copies of this book, contact:
Xlibris Corporation
1-888-795-4274
www.Xlibris.com
Orders@Xlibris.com
112523

Much love to my daughters Danielle and Alisha, for their support

&

Many thanks to my editor and friend, Charles F. Finley, Jr.

CHAPTER 1

As a child, if I was nervous or afraid of something, I would sometimes make up songs to sing and poems to write. I loved music and poetry, whether I made it up or just heard a song playing on the radio, or if I read a beautiful, meaningful poem in a magazine, in a newspaper, or in a book. Songs and poems were the perfect reflection of my emotions. The same is true today. Right now, I can hear music playing with a chorus of melodic harmony in a sweet country song. It sounds like the chords are playing on a well-made guitar with its very perfect, distinctive sounds; as, the strings of a banjo are strummed along with it. I've never heard that song before, and I've never heard anything sung quite like it. The slow rhythm is one that I will never forget. It's all so fitting right now since I'm down by the river. I lie here feeling bruised and beaten, unable to do anything except remember; as, the music keeps playing while I keep singin' in my mind:

Floatin', goin' . . .

Floatin' on down the river.

Downstream, upstream . . .

The water sure makes me quiver.

Leavin', goin' . . .

I might go on forever.

See me, hear me . . .

The ferocious waves are tryin' to pierce my soul,

As I'm tossed against these rocks.

The timeless river's got a hold on me,

But in the end—I decide what will be.

This ol' endless river's going to set me free.

See me, hear me—know that . . .

One day, we'll be together.

I look up high at the big blue sky . . .

It takes my blues away.

Come embrace me now, my kindred soul.

Will you take me now—this way?

Come grace me now with your love so deep.

Please hear me when I cry.

See me, hear me . . .

'cause I might be coming home today.

I can see that it's turning dark now and the temperature is much cooler, so it must be nearing sunset. That's not saying a whole lot considering the unpredictable weather in good ol' Virginia. I do know that the springtime temperatures are warm during the day and much cooler at night. Based on that, I believe that it's still spring. I can hear the leaves rubbing briskly together as they move against the tree limbs. I can hear all the whispers stirring around in the howling wind and my head is spinning like a whirlpool. I can hear the sounds of night owls. I lie here, uncertain of where the hell I am or how long I've been here or why I'm here. I only know that I'm here, feeling helpless, in the hands of one of the great rivers.

What I do know is that it's the time of day when most people wouldn't want to be alone. Am I really alone or is someone or something evil, crawling, walking, or just lurking around nearby—sneering, snickering at me because my fate lies in their hands? What can I do if something or someone comes after me?

I don't hear any peculiar sounds, so maybe my imagination is running away with me. Maybe no one is close by or, even if there is, maybe they do want to help me. Maybe there was someone with me when I first got here. If that's the case, where are they now? I want answers to what I need to know.

I'm so tired and this throbbing pain in my head just won't go away. I can barely see what's around me with my blurred vision, except for the water and the patches of woods surrounding the river and the sky. Everything looks so distorted and I'm bleeding. Why?

Right now, I feel as though I'm at a standstill with all the twists and turns of time—a past with sometimes unending turmoil consumed by anger and tears; but, I also know in my heart, that I must have felt some happiness in my life. I just have to believe this. I dread the thought of someone leaving me here, dwindling away like this. Maybe it was accidental, or maybe I did this to myself. Will anyone even notice that I'm gone? If they do, will they search for me? I'm so confused.

I want to get up and run, but I can't because I can barely move my legs. They won't bend or turn in any direction unless they glide along with the current of the river water. I can't move my feet at all. There's no feeling—no cramping; no twitching, or erratic movements. I can't even wiggle my toes. Oh no . . . I can't sit up. I do recall a time when doctors told me that temporary paralysis might occur, but for what reasons? Right now—I don't even know. There might be more physically wrong with me than I even realize. I wonder if I can speak. Should I yell or could that be a grave mistake? I just have to try.

"Hello? Is anybody there? Hello . . . hello. Can anyone hear me?"

Well, that didn't do me any good at all. At least I know that I can speak, even though the sound of my voice wasn't heard by anyone.

I'm feeling useless. The water is cold, but luckily, I'm only partially adrift in shallow water. One of my arms is caught in something so I haven't started floatin' away. This vast river hasn't tried to devour me yet, but the water's current is slowly starting to increase in strength and the level is starting to rise. I hope to be rescued before the water starts gushing, and before it turns so dark out here that I can't see anything at all—but if that doesn't happen, I refuse to be afraid.

I remember my earlier years clearly, but why can't I remember what I've done today or where I've been recently? Do I have some form of amnesia, too?

This time conscious world seems to have come to an abrupt halt for me. I wonder if this is the last place that I'll ever see. At this moment, I want time to go on endlessly. How much weakness and pain does a person have to endure? I hope my pain will go away. All people have to do is to find their inner strength and courage deep within themselves. How will I find my inner strength? Do I make a wish? Do I just hope? Do I pray? I feel so alone. Reaching for the depths of my inner emotions, my deepest thoughts, my most treasured times, might help me to feel strong again, and like I can survive whatever obstacles cross my path. I have to remember all that I can since it might be the glue that will keep my mind together.

Overcome by weakness, Rae Ann's head tilted to one side on the harsh dirt that scratched her and penetrated into her pores, and into the deep cuts on her face, as she lay near the shallow edge of the river. Uncontrollably, she closed her eyes and then she was flooded with the memories from her past. In her mind, she envisioned and thought to herself . . . I still remember most of my early childhood years when my life was filled with zest. Life was nearly perfect in my eyes back then, but I also remember the saddest times.

There was the time when our mama left, but even so, my older brother Ray, and my younger sister Sue, knew that she'd always come back to Virginia, whether it was for a visit or to stay. We knew even then, that she loved us in the only way that she knows how to. It's always been that way. Although we were saddened, we understood that there were reasons why she left in the first place.

My daddy was a brave navy man who died when he was very young. Mama said things were just too hard on her and that she didn't want to raise children without a husband. After daddy died, she still stayed with us for a while, but then she moved away and our grandma and granddaddy told us that they were going to take care of us. I still loved our mama and so did Ray and Sue, but we all understood that she wanted more in life than what she had in our home here in Virginia. Our grandparents said that someday, she would learn and understand what family is truly all about. They said that she was just too young right now.

CHAPTER 2

Some of our best times as children were when our family would pack up our things and jump into the Plymouth. When Ray, and Sue, and I rode in that old sleek, stylish car, we thought it was as good as riding in a fancy Cadillac. We thought our family was rich and had it all.

Life was great back in the sixties, especially when we rode to Caroline County; a big part of the countryside. Our great-grandparents' home would always be our first stop in Port Royal, VA.

Once there, my cousin Willie, who was also visiting, and I, loved to run to where the swings were—behind an old vacant building. They appeared as if they hung from the beautiful, blue sky because they were so lengthy. We'd sit in those swings and pretend like we were trying to see angels. We'd reach high, up to the often speckled, white, dusted clouds. They weren't anything but peaceful remedies for an unsettled soul and an aching heart. I'd look up at all its natural beauty, and I couldn't help but smile and feel the peace and tranquility that the sky offers. Sometimes, I felt as though I wanted to become a part of it all forever.

I still remember on a particular September day, when Willie said "It's a sunny, fine day out here, and I know that you want to swing and look at the sky all day, Rae Ann, but don't you think we need to get back to great grandma's? It's almost time to eat."

Willie clearly expressed his point-of-view when he felt strongly about something back then, and he always wanted to keep his feet planted firmly on the ground. I was a focused child who often loved to dream and imagine.

"Okay Willie boy, I'm ready to go now."

Then we left the swings, walked to the gas station, and opened the big chest filled with drinks. We only paid twenty-five cents for a drink back then. After drinking it, we always made sure to save the empty bottles for the nickel deposit during those frugal times. After leaving the gas station, we'd walk back to the house, never suspecting that anything could or would ever scare us out there during the light of day or at night; that is, until I learned about some bone-chilling, frightful times that happened.

At night, the grownups usually sat inside the house, and the rest of us sat on a screened porch facing the narrow road. There were many large trees that stood tall in the front yard and along the sides of the road, with the rattling sounds of their branches and leaves. Cousin Charles told us that if we walked off the porch into the yard, the night would swallow us up whole. We'd be blinded by the darkness and unable to see, and we wouldn't know where to go, and then the bats would get us. They'd just swoop down from where they clung on those big ol' heavy branches, aim right for our heads, and get tangled in our hair and carry us away; therefore, we never left the porch at night unless one of the grownups were with us. Silly little Willie used to bet me a quarter that I wouldn't leave the porch. He was right about that. He could keep his ol' quarter because I wasn't about to leave the porch. Back then, a quarter was a whole lot of money to us kids. It was a tempting offer, but I wouldn't do it—not even for a shiny quarter.

When we were called in for the night, we usually sat around in the warm, cozy living room near the pot-belly stove and watch scary movies on the black and white television until we fell asleep.

The next morning, after eating a big breakfast, we said our good-byes to those who planned to remain at our great-grandparents' home. The rest of us eagerly jumped in the cars and headed for Milford for our next exciting visit.

When arriving at our cousins' home, we'd run to the backyard where we knew our cousins would be. We were always so excited to go there because when it turned dark outdoors, we knew that Willie and Charles were going to tell us some spooky stories to scare the daylights out of us. Nothing could compare to the stories that they told. It was what most of us liked best. I know they enjoyed telling their stories as much as we enjoyed listening to them. It didn't matter if anyone believed their stories or not because we all were entranced by the way the stories were told. Especially when told by Willie, who had a way to make the stories sound very real; the way he changed the sound of his voice, and the way he acted, with the many looks on his face.

The grownups, again, always went inside, but the screen door was left unlocked and the wooden door would always stay open so they could keep an eye on us.

My cousins and I always sat in a circle around a big campfire that Uncle Russ built for us. There were sounds of the crackling wood, along with the colors from the flickering flames. The light from the fire was just enough for us to see each of our faces. The shadows made enormous silhouettes on the house in the night, and set the mood for a night of chilling storytelling. Our younger cousins sat closely to the older cousins, where they felt safe in the darkness. We all sat in anticipation, just waiting and wondering what the boys were going to say.

On this September night, as we sat waiting for the stories to be told, we noticed that Willie and Charles had stone cold looks on their faces. They gazed into the fire, and then at all of us.

Willie said, "The stories that we have to tell y'all tonight will affect your entire lives. I'm not kidding. You all have to listen to what we have to say to you very carefully, because it is very important. These stories are scary and they're all true. Don't ever forget it."

Charles and Willie looked at us with such seriousness that none of us cracked a smile on our faces. Charles spoke.

"Well, I'm going to tell y'all the first story and here it goes . . .

On one dark, dismal night, when there wasn't a star to be seen up in the sky in our town of Bowling Green—a young girl, who was just as pretty as she could be, left her home to meet her boyfriend. Her mama and daddy didn't approve of her seeing him and felt that she was barely old enough to even have a boyfriend. Her daddy told her that she had plenty of time left in her life to have a boyfriend, so she didn't need to rush. Well, her name was Mary. Do y'all remember Mary, here in Bowling Green? Well anyway, Mary had her own opinion about it and expressed it to her daddy, and now I'm goin' to tell you what her last conversation with her daddy was.

"Daddy, in your opinion I might barely be old enough, but still, I am old enough, so that's the point and I'll see y'all later. Bye daddy. Bye mama."

Her daddy said, "Mary, don't go. I mean it. It's dark and it's late and it's getting ready to storm out there. The bats will get you, so you better stay here. You can go out tomorrow."

Mary said, "Daddy, I'm not falling for that story anymore. The bats don't weigh enough to carry me away anywhere. I've got to go. If I don't go right now, I'll be late. Bye daddy." Then she gave her daddy a hug, and gave her mama a hug, and told them that she'd be back home about 9:30 pm.

Well, you know 9:30 pm came and Mary wasn't home yet. It was indeed, a thunderous, stormy night. Then, midnight came and there was still no sign of Mary.

Her mama and daddy were very worried about her, so her daddy said, "I told her it was going to storm. Listen to that thunder! The lightning bolts have hit some trees! She'll be scared and she won't know what to do. I'll bet she didn't even think about that. That boy must be pretty important to her—for her to have gone out in this mess. I'll go try to find her." Then he left and drove around the town in the almost blinding rain. He knew his daughter wouldn't like him checking up on her, but he went to her boyfriend's home anyway. Her boyfriend's name was Andy. Andy heard the doorbell and he answered the door.

"Where's Mary? She never came home. She's here with you, isn't she Andy?"

Andy scratched his head, as if he was trying to think. "You mean she didn't stay home with you tonight? Then he looked at Mary's father with a curious look and said, "I don't know where she is then."

Mary's daddy wasn't sure if he should believe him or not and said, "What do you mean, boy? She has to be with you! This isn't funny. Are you tryin' to play some kind of game with me?"

"No sir. I wouldn't do that, especially if it has anything to do with Mary."

"Well, something must have happened to my daughter and we better find her."

He thought about searching Andy's home by himself, but instead he called the police. A search was performed; not only there, but everywhere that they thought Mary could be. There was still no sign of Mary and there weren't any clues. She just vanished! To this day, we believe that the bats were big enough and strong enough to actually carry her away. Poor, poor Mary never was found."

"Well, she didn't sit on a porch with a screen, so she wasn't protected," commented my cousin Dawn, feeling confident that she knew this for a fact.

"Dawn, have you noticed that we're not sittin' on a porch with a screen on it right now, either?" asked Willie. "Are you scared? Oh, look behind you Dawn 'cause I think I see something comin' at ya right now. You better run while you can! Woooo Dawn! Are you leavin' us?"

"Stop it Willie!" Then Dawn, looking all around her, got up and bolted over to Willie's side and said, "If I go, I ain't goin' alone 'cause where I go, you'll go. I'll grab your hand and you'll be carried away with me!"

Anna, one of my younger cousins, age four at that time, looked and said, "Y'all stop 'cause I'm scared."

Marie, who was five years old back then, was afraid too, but she also wanted to stay outdoors with everyone.

"You don't have to go inside right now Anna or you either Marie, because we're safe out here. Willie was just playin' around; besides, daddy told us before, that the light from the fire will keep bats away," commented cousin Francis.

Then Charles said, "Willie will tell the second story. Now, if you younger ones don't feel that y'all can handle it, you should go inside right now."

Surprisingly, none of the younger ones got up, and neither did we, even though we shook from head to toe, feeling intense fear. We no longer felt the safety or security in our surroundings.

Willie said, "All right you all get a grip now and stay close together. I have something to add about the bats around here that you've all been hearing about for a long time. Y'all know those roads about five blocks from here?

Well, two more people, we believe, were swooped up by the bats a few months ago. Your cousin Charles had a run-in with those ol' bats too. They had him dangling in the air, and he did some sort of somersault and broke away from 'em one night, ended up hanging upside down from a branch up in the trees, by the bow made from his shoe laces. He hollered for help, as he swayed back and forth in the air for about an hour, until finally somebody heard him and got him down. Now, you know Charles ain't afraid of anything, but let me tell you—after that, he was shook up for a long time. He doesn't even want to go back there anymore. It was a traumatizing experience for my poor older brother. Ain't that right Charles?"

"Willie!" exclaimed Charles, who looked like he couldn't contain his emotions any longer. He smiled and said "Woo boy," and then he laughed. That was when the rest of us caught on to what Willie was trying to make us believe the entire time.

Dawn asked, "Willie was any of it true at all?"

"Heck no! Charles don't know how to do a somersault and he didn't dangle in the air from bats carrying him away, but I really had y'all goin' for a couple of minutes—didn't I? I wish that you all could see the looks on your faces. You all believed every word of it."

"Willie! You rascal! Did Charles know that you were going to tell us that story?"

"Well yeah, we planned it out in the car on the way back here from great grandma's house."

"Thank goodness that story wasn't true," one of them remarked.

They all looked at each other and laughed and laughed until Willie's and Charles's expressions changed on their faces again. That's when we knew they were going to tell us another story, and we knew that it was probably something that really did happen.

Willie said, "It is unfortunate that the story about Mary, and the story that I'm about to tell you concerning another missing boy who was never found, are both true."

Then looking solemnly into each of our bewildered, frenzied-struck faces, Willie clasped his hands together and then told the story like he'd never done before. This particular story was told with genuine concern.

"Okay now, we're not going to joke anymore tonight during our storytelling time with y'all. I'm going to tell what happened last year, and I urge all of you to take me seriously."

"I assure you that every one of us will take you and Charles seriously, Willie."

Francis knew by the tone of her little brother's voice that he meant business. There was no doubt of how strongly he felt about informing his relatives and others of the strange occurrences.

Willie began to tell the story.

"A couple of boys from the school that Charles goes to, left school one day and decided to go to our Aunt Millie's house. If Charles and me only knew that they were headed over there, we would've put a stop to what they were doing *real* quick. Anyway, they went over there because one of the boys said that he was hungry. The boy that was hungry was a mean boy named Randy. He was a bully and he still is. The other boy's name is Mike. Y'all might already know who Randy is, 'cause his name pops up a lot in the neighborhood and we don't get along with that boy at all."

Charles then added, "Naw, we don't get along with him and let me tell you—nobody else in Caroline or anywhere else gets along with him as far as that goes."

Willie said, "Well, that's true. Like I said, he's a bully and he's mean and hateful to everybody."

Then he looked directly into each of our eyes and reminded us to remember this story, too. His brothers, sisters, cousins, and friends all agreed to never forget any of the stories that they were told. Cousin Lori shook her head up and down, a bit impatiently.

"Willie, believe me! We're not ever going to forget. We promise. Now go ahead. You know I'm anxious and I'm afraid that mama will tell us to go inside before you're finished. I don't want to miss anything and I don't want to have to wait for another week or two before we can hear the rest of the story."

"Okay, okay, Lori. You proved your point, but it's important that y'all take in every single word I say and take heed, because it might be a matter of life or death someday."

Willie continued the story . . . "Randy told Mike to go with him to Aunt Millie's."

Mike asked, "Why do you want to go over there, Randy? I think we better stay here at school."

Randy answered, "I'm hungry and I don't want to go there by myself. Come on now."

"You know they don't want anybody there when they're not home—*especially not you*. They know that you do things that get you and others in trouble. Hey Randy? Look here; I've got some money. I can buy you some snacks and we can eat right here at school."

"I don't like what they're havin' for lunch, and I don't want any snacks. Don't you worry about what that family thinks of me, either! They're not even goin' to know we're there, so we ain't goin' to get caught."

"How do you know, Randy?"

"'Cause nobody's home, so nobody will see us, goofball. You don't know for a fact, that they would mind us being there, anyway. Listen now, what if I tell you that I might be friends with them now?"

"You're friends with them now, Randy?" asked Mike.

"Yeah, I'm friends with them now. They just didn't have a chance to tell you 'cause you haven't seen them for a while. Don't you worry about a thing, Mike."

"Umm . . . I don't know about that Randy. I've never done anything like this before."

Randy looked at him, as he grabbed Mike's collar, and pulled him along side of him and said, "Well, you're going to do it today, so come on!" He had a threatening look on his face as if he dared for Mike to say one disagreeable word to him. He looked and sounded so angry, and at that moment, Mike didn't say a word that would upset Randy.

"All right, I'm goin' with you, but I don't like it, and I'm never going anywhere with you again." Mike was starting to feel nervous and uneasy.

Willie said the two boys then walked to our Aunt Millie's and Uncle Warren's home. When they got there, something was caught in the door and it kept it from closing tightly. Randy smiled because he knew they'd have no problem getting in. Once inside, Randy smugly sounded with a . . . "Hmmm! Well, *look'a there*. We can just walk on in and walk out of here, just as we please. You'd think that people would want to make sure their doors are really locked."

Mike felt sick and looked a little perplexed; as, he just stared at Randy for a couple of seconds. He wondered if Randy had already been there that day and rigged the door. Randy probably planned everything.

"Mike, why don't you go in the kitchen and look in the fridge? I want you to see what they've got to eat. I'm goin' to take a look out here to make sure nobody's comin', and then I'll come back and get some food." Then, Randy stepped outside and Mike opened the refrigerator door and yelled just as loud as he could, and Randy came runnin' back inside the kitchen. Then, Mike turned around, facing Randy with a petrified look, and then, almost bumping into Randy, he started to run. Randy looked at what was inside the refrigerator, and then he turned around with a wicked look in his eyes and ran after Mike. Mike dashed out the house, ran down the road, and then toward the swings behind the vacant building in Port Royal. Randy was still right there behind him. Mike stopped and stood there, trying to catch his breath and looked up at Randy who was only standing an inch or two away from him.

"Randy, did you know that hog's head was in the refrigerator? It still has its eyes, and they stared right at me! Did you put it there to scare me?"

Randy leaned over, even closer to Mike, and asked "What are you talkin' about Mike? I was just as spoofed as you. I've been with you most of the day. There was no time to do anything like that."

Mike, in disbelief answered, "I didn't see you until after class. I don't think anybody saw you in class. Were you just hangin' around outside?"

"What do you mean Mike? You saw me at school. You can't deny that. As far as you know, I was in class."

Mike thought for a moment or two and answered Randy by saying, "I didn't see you **inside** the school though. You know that I first saw you on the schoolyard."

Randy said, "What difference does that make? It was still on school property."

"Well, did the teachers see you in class?"

"I never thought about that Mike. Why don't you believe that my teacher saw me in class? Are you planning to tell my teacher? What are you plannin' to do Mike?"

"Uh, I don't know, you're pretty sneaky."

Mike didn't like the way Randy looked at him after he made that remark. He shook, and folded his arms tightly, squeezing them; as, he looked downward at the ground, digging his shoe nervously into the dirt. He really didn't know what to do. There was no place for him to run. I just know that he couldn't get away from Randy.

"What the real truth is, we might not ever know," said Willie, now with his head facing downward, and his eyes closed, thought about the incident. He hated Randy.

Then slowly, while lifting his head as he widened his eyes and looked closely, at his cousins, noticing the concerned expressions on all their faces with their glassy eyes, said, "No one ever saw or heard from Mike again.

This was another one of the saddest times our town has ever had. It's another unsolved puzzle. We only know what Randy told the police and what we believe really happened."

Charles added, "Randy talks about it a lot, like it's no big deal."

"Now, let me ask each of y'all . . . do you think that those two boys had a guilty conscience for being where they had no business being in the first place? Naw, not Randy. He doesn't have a guilty conscience about anything that he does wrong, but maybe Mike did. I believe that Mike was scared half to death. You know that Mike didn't even want to be there. He was a nice boy. A lot of people miss him. I don't know what your opinion is after hearing this story, but I think Randy had planned everything. He admitted to the police that he and Mike played hooky from school and that he was with Mike at the playground. He told them that they were playing on the swings and he looked away for just a minute, turned around, and Mike had disappeared. The police didn't do anything to him. He didn't even get punished for playing hooky from school or for breaking into Aunt Millie and Uncle Warren's home. The adults decided that he had already suffered, and felt that he had been punished enough because of what happened to his friend. Now, let me ask you this . . . do any one of you think for even a minute that Randy was really a friend of Mike's? Naw, he wasn't his friend. He wasn't ever Mike's friend. Randy fooled everybody. He fooled Mike's parents, the police, our family; everybody. Ever since that happened, there's been stories at our school about the hog's head in the refrigerator and that there was a curse on it and that the curse caused Mike's disappearance, but I know that Randy had something to do with it."

Today, as Rae Ann meshed with the memories of that night long ago, she thought to herself . . . I told Willie that I believed Randy had something to do with it, too, and that I just didn't understand why he wasn't arrested for what he did. They should have put him away, locked him up in a jail cell, and they should have thrown away the key right then. Randy once said that his daddy told him and his brother to show people who's boss around here. They'd step in anyone's way and do whatever they wanted to do to get what they wanted, no matter what. Rae Ann thought back to what Willie said that same night, long ago—about Randy.

"The police never found enough proof of what really happened. They didn't think a little boy could or would concoct a story like that—certainly not a young country boy. Since there had been other disappearances, you know—like Mary, they assumed that someone else had done it. They felt they had no choice but to believe Randy's story. This all happened to Mike about six months ago."

Willie told us what happened to the very first ones that were ever reported missing in their neighborhood.

"Daddy said that the very first two disappearances that he knows about happened right after I was born. Mama and daddy had two friends. I think mama said their names were Joey and Elsie. They wanted to see me after I was brought home from the hospital. They never made it to the house, though. Mama and daddy don't talk much about it *a' tall* anymore. All I know is that nobody was ever arrested for their disappearance, either.

Now, I have one last story to tell tonight. I know you might be scared, but let me emphasize again, how very important it is, for me to tell you about this. This is serious business. I know it's a whole lot to remember, but it might help somehow in the future."

All of them held tightly to each other's hands at that point.

Lori looked at Willie.

"Well, here we go again." She rolled her eyes upward and shook her head from side to side as she thought about how it was a waste of their time, to make sure that they would remember all these stories.

Did she really take what her cousins Willie and Charles said seriously, or did she think that they were only stories that she enjoyed listening to? He only wanted them all to be careful, and to remember, because he didn't want anything terrible to ever happen to them. Either way, she still answered as the others had, although her anxiousness and impatience had shown.

"We promise that we'll remember," were the words that echoed from each of them.

"All right now, let me tell you all about the mysterious, gruesome, creepy night. This is another true story, and it's about another difficult time that we've all experienced here in the county. It's been said that what really happened at this particular time is difficult to determine too."

Francis stood up and said, "Hold on Willie. I think Miranda and I better get Anna and Marie inside first. They've heard more than enough scary stories tonight. We probably should have made them go in earlier. I'm surprised that they're not scared out of their wits. We were told that they are supposed to be inside by 8:00 tonight and I know it's close to that time now."

A few minutes later, Miranda and our cousin Francis got back outside and sat down.

"Hey! We didn't miss anything did we?"

"No, we wouldn't start the story without y'all. Now, let me start by saying that I don't know if any of you have thought about it, but none of us have gone swimming or fishing in the pond, or for any walks for quite some time on our dirt roads in the woods, or even near the woods. We haven't even walked over there when it's light outdoors, and y'all know that it's a good shortcut to use when you need to go to the market. Well, that's out of the question too. We can't hang out by the creek either. There are a few reasons for this.

One night, when it was dark and late, two teenage girls and one teenage boy from around here were walkin' on one of the dirt roads. It was already past time for them to be home and they knew it, but they were having so much fun, that they didn't even worry about the time. They were laughin' and carryin' on and one of the girls jumped up on the boy's back. He gave her a piggyback ride and those two laughed some more, and they were flirtin' with each other, and didn't think about how far ahead they were from the other girl—until it was too late. They called for her, but there was no answer. They walked all the way back, tracing their footsteps to where they first started walking, in hopes of finding her. They thought that maybe she headed back to where they were before they went into the woods. But they saw no signs of her anywhere until the boy looked around and saw one of their friend's shoes. The shoe was still partially laced and was tangled up on a small limb that barely hung from a small branch on a leafless, half-dead skeleton of a bush. A little farther down the path, were small puddles of blood. They were really scared, and decided to go home. They ran pretty far, but the girl and boy got tired. Then they stopped to rest for a few minutes. Once they found a large, thick, branch to sit on, they heard some noise and called out to the other girl; assuming that it was her. She didn't answer back, and they didn't know what to do. So, then the one girl that the boy was with, whose name was Catherine, told the boy, whose name was Danny, that he should check where the sound was coming from, but he didn't want to leave her in the woods alone. He thought it might be someone else there or something else makin' that noise. Then she insisted that he go without her because their friend might be nearby. Catherine thought that maybe their friend just strayed, got lost, and couldn't find her way back to where they were. He thought she might be right about this, so he started to walk away from her. Suddenly, he heard an unusual sound—like something was moving. He could hear the crunching sounds of branches and of the dry leaves that were scattered. He knew what that sound was, because he had walked on fallen branches many times, and they'd snap into smaller pieces. He knew that she wanted him to leave, but first he turned around, and looked back to where he left his friend Catherine, and it was no surprise that she wasn't anywhere in sight either. She disappeared—just like their other friend!

Things keep happening this way. You can't take your eyes off the one you're with—not even for a second! He tried to tell her that he was afraid that something could happen to her, too, if they separated! Why didn't she listen to him? Why did he listen to her? He called out her name, but there was no answer. His heart thumped and he panicked and decided to get out of there. Once out of the woods, he'd go get help.

That boy was one lucky boy! He did make it out of the woods in one piece. He was scared to death, but he was alive. He called for help. As always, there were police and search parties, and lots of town folks trying to help, too, but the two young girls were never seen again.

Now, we know that the big, black bats with their pointy fangs and their big claws have swooped up more girls than boys, but do you really think the bats did it, or do you think it could have been a person? Danny believes that a mean, vicious person did it. We've given this spooky person a name. We call him the *Dirt Man*. It had to be the *Dirt Man* that was hidden in the dark shadows by the trees.

Daddy told us about Danny, Catherine, and the other girl. He told us that it didn't happen that long ago, and that the police need to collect more clues and gather more facts together before they can go public with the information. As a matter of fact, it was just a few weeks ago that it all happened. Daddy told me that we might know them personally, that's why he didn't tell us what their names are. They don't want us to be upset, so they're not going to tell us anything much about it right now. One thing is for sure though, my daddy said that the woods are off limits to all children, considering how unsafe they are, and if we even think about going near that area, we can forget it unless an adult is with us."

By the time Willie finished telling the last story that night, our parents called all of us in for the remainder of the evening. Uncle Russ came out and put out the fire.

"You look pretty shaken Dawn. Did the boys scare you?"

"Yes. They scared everybody. Do our friends have to walk home by themselves?"

"No, I reckon I can take them home in the truck. Tell them to climb in, 'cause we'll have to go now. It's dark and it's startin' to get late. I've got other things to do."

"Okay, thanks, daddy."

Russ drove all of them home and then he went back home.

There were so many great times with all the relatives. I don't believe any of us will ever forget that night or any other day that we spent together. We enjoyed each other's company every time we were together. There was never anything better than living life in the country.

CHAPTER 3

Four more months passed, and it was then January. We spent our days going to school, riding our bicycles, seeing our relatives, and sometimes my cousins and I would help by getting the soil ready for gardening.

One day, when I was covered from head to toe with dirt, Charles and Willie looked at me and I just knew that they were up to some mischief.

"Hey Willie . . . I think our cousin could use a little water 'cause with all that dirt on her, she could probably grow something."

"Yeah Charles, she could probably use a lot of water."

Then out came the water hose. Those mischievous cousins of mine, just as sly as they could be took the hose and sprayed me with that cold water. There I stood, drenched with those two silly boys grinning from ear to ear. It sure didn't stop me from taking that hose from them and spraying them, too.

"Well, at least we're all clean now. I hear there's a party goin' on tonight, but I don't think we'll be able to go. It's a shame too, since we're all cleaned up and all we need to do is put our good clothes on."

"You're right, but we can still have some fun. We can play some music and dance a little. It'll be almost as good as being there."

Uncle Russ, Aunt Maggie, Aunt Millie and Uncle Warren, my grandma, my granddaddy, and lots of other relatives planned to go to a party at the Tallhouse family's farmhouse in Milford. We couldn't persuade them to let us go to the party with them. Grandma said only grownups could go and children fifteen and older could attend. She said that I could spend the night with my cousins since I couldn't go to the party. Charles and Francis and a couple of the others had their own plans, but I knew that it would be fun to hang out with Willie. He was my closest cousin. It was the next best thing to going to the party, so I had no complaints at all. I wondered who was going to stay with us most of the night though. Then I found out that Uncle Russ had called Miranda. Willie and I just smiled at the thought of Miranda staying with us. The grownups all thought that Miranda was a *sweet little angel*. Little did they know about how sneaky she was and this night was to be no exception.

Russ, Maggie, and the others left and the first thing that Miranda did was give us something to drink. She said she didn't want us to get thirsty before we got there.

"Miranda? After we get where?" She had Willie and I puzzled.

After that, she looked at us, grinning from ear to ear, and asked "How would y'all like to go to the party?"

Willie looked at her and asked "Are you crazy girl? You know we're not supposed to go any parties tonight. We ain't even supposed to leave the house. Have you forgotten what's been going on around here? We can't go anywhere at night without an adult and we sure can't walk anywhere."

"Willie boy, show some respect. I'm not crazy. I've made some plans for us and as far as our safety; we don't have to worry about walking there because we'll have a car. I'm going to call Mary Beth. Mary Beth is an adult by law. She's eighteen years old."

"Ooooh boy! Let's go then. You can count on me, Miranda. How about you Rae Ann? Rae Ann, you don't have to worry about Francis telling on us 'cause she's already gone to another party. You were in the kitchen when she told me what she was goin' to be doin' tonight, and Dawn is at the Rollison's home with them and their little girl. I'm not sure where Charles is goin' to be."

"All right Willie, if you don't think we'll get caught—you can count me in, too."

"What if mama or daddy sees us there, Miranda?" asked Willie.

"Willie boy, you are always worrying about something, but to answer your question, I've got it all planned out. We're not going to hang out in the same rooms as everybody else. You know how big that house is. We're going to meet up with some of our friends and cousins on the third floor."

"Okay then, I just wanted to make sure, Miranda, 'cause you know it'll be hell to pay if my daddy catches us over there."

"Willie, what kind of language are you using little boy?" Then she giggled and said "I didn't know you had it in you Willie—to talk that way."

Rae Ann said, "Miranda, you know that Willie talks like my Uncle Russ sometimes."

"Well, it makes no difference to me anyway," replied Miranda.

"Y'all just hurry up and get ready now."

Willie said "I'm ready now, but let me tell you something—I ain't no little boy, Miranda."

Then Rae Ann said "I'm ready too. Willie, don't mind her."

"Hey Rae Ann, let's go in the den and talk for a few minutes."

Rae Ann motioned for Willie to walk closer to her because she didn't want Miranda to hear what she was about to ask Willie.

"Hey Willie, let me ask you, are you sure we should do this? Grandma and granddaddy won't let me stay here for a solid month if they find out."

"Miranda's not going to let us get caught, Rae Ann 'cause if we're caught, that would mean that she's caught too, and she ain't goin' to let that happen."

"Well, then Willie, let's go to the party."

"You can bet on that, cousin."

About half an hour went by and then Mary Beth pulled up in her Firebird. Miranda and Mary Beth told Willie and Rae Ann to go ahead and get in the car because it was finally time to leave for their night of fun.

Miranda asked "Hey, do y'all really want to get brave and have some excitement?"

"What do ya mean Miranda?" Rae Ann wanted to know exactly what they planned to do that night.

"I mean, we're goin' to take a shortcut through the woods down the road that goes through there."

Willie felt chills move up and down his spine. He was leery of going to the party now. His feelings of excitement turned into anxiety and fear. "This is kinda creepy. I don't think I want to go that way at all. You know the rules Miranda!"

"Willie, I'm the babysitter and I'm making the decisions tonight, and I've already decided that we're all goin' to the party, and I don't want to hear another word about it!"

"Shame on you Miranda! The grownups would be disappointed in your behavior."

"Don't worry Willie. "We'll be out of there in a flash." said Mary Beth. Then she started driving in the direction of the party on the bumpy road deep inside the mysterious woods. Willie and Rae Ann felt like they were there for eternity. The long winding road curved around like a serpent slithering in the night, and the sounds of the wildlife that crept, weaving between the dark, hovering trees were enough to send anyone running without hesitation, back to safety in their own homes.

"Listen to those animals chattering like crazy."

"It doesn't sound like it's just animals chattering to me. That noise sounds like whispers. There's probably people out here," said Willie, as he continued to listen attentively, heeding every sound as if it were some sort of warning to them of what lies ahead of them during the night.

Rae Ann said "How much longer is it going to be before we get to the house? I don't like it here at all."

"I don't like it at all either, cousin," remarked Willie. "What if the *Dirt Man* comes out and snatches us up? I forgot how big those trees are. A person could hide behind one of those trees and no one could ever see who it is. What if one of those giant bats flies out from one of those tree branches? What if they bite us with their fangs?"

"It'll just be about ten more minutes or so y'all, so shush now. I think we've heard enough. I was supposed to meet Sammy out here, but so far, I don't see him anywhere. We'll just sit here in my car for a couple of minutes and wait for him. He needs to hurry and get here 'cause I'm almost out of gas and my car doesn't sound right. I've been havin' some problems with it lately. I guess

I better not leave the motor running." Then Mary Beth turned the key to turn off the ignition.

"Shhhh" . . . whispered Miranda, "don't tell them that you've been having car problems 'cause you'll really scare 'em and we'll never hear the end of it."

"It's too late now. You've already said it. Do you mean to tell us that you got us out here in these spooky woods in a broken down car?" asked Rae Ann.

"Yeah, don't even try to get out of it Miranda. You and Mary Beth need to turn this car around and take Rae Ann and me back to my home right now 'cause I know that you've both lost your minds!" Willie shouted with an angered voice. "We don't want anybody snatchin' us tonight. It's no tellin' where we'll end up."

"It's not broken down. We got this far didn't we?" asked Miranda.

"I think he's right, Miranda. Things aren't turning out the way we planned," Mary Beth remarked, feeling some disappointment about the way things were turning out.

"Oh, you're just mad 'cause Sammy didn't show up. We'll be at the house in just a few more minutes," said Miranda. "Now let me ask you somethin' Willie boy. Do you really want to go all the way back through these woods? It would take about twenty more minutes or even longer to get back through these woods, so what do y'all children really want to do?"

"Who are you callin' children Miranda? You're not a grownup yet. You're not eighteen years old yet," said Willie in a defensive tone of voice.

"Listen, we don't have time for this," said Mary Beth. "Just hurry up and make a decision so we can get going."

"Oh Willie, let's just go ahead and go to the party. At least we'll be near our folks," said Rae Ann.

"Yeah, okay then, let's get goin'," said Willie.

So Mary Beth started the car again and it slowly sputtered, as something spurted out from underneath it. It continued to move down the road, with its grinding, screeching sounds until it just stalled. Mary Beth was able to start it up again, but then it came to a sudden halt and made no sound at all.

"Uh oh," said Mary Beth.

Miranda said, "What do you mean—uh oh?"

"Oh no!" groaned Willie. "Is the car completely broken down now?"

"I'm afraid so, Willie," replied Miranda. "We'll just get out of the car, hold hands, and walk. It won't take us long since we don't have much farther to go."

"Oh naw, naw . . . naw!" exclaimed Willie as he vented his anger. "This can't be happening to us tonight!"

Rae Ann said, "I feel the same way Willie. Listen though—you can hold my hand."

"That's good, 'cause I'm not about to hold Miranda's or Mary Beth's hands. *It's no tellin'* what will happen to us if we hold their hands. Are you sure the car is broken down? Maybe we can work on it a little bit. I think I know a little something about fixin' cars. I help daddy sometimes."

Mary Beth said, "I'm sure there's something wrong with it. This has happened before. It's no use trying to fix it little Willie boy. It needs to be put in the shop. You are *just too cute for askin' though.* Ain't that right, Miranda? Isn't he just the cutest little thing?"

Miranda was already aggravated and blamed Mary Beth. She then answered Mary Beth by replying, "Oh, just shut up, Mary Beth. Why didn't you tell me that your car is just a piece of junk?"

She looked away from Miranda and spoke to Willie and Rae Ann.

"Nothing bad has happened to us yet, so don't assume that anything terrible is goin' to happen to us now, Willie. Do you understand that, too, Rae Ann? You two can hold each other hands, but y'all will still have to walk with us. We all need to stay together. All right now, let's get out of the car now and start walking. We're wasting time."

"That's fine with us," replied Rae Ann and then she said, "It'll be harder to lose each other that way."

So the four of them got out of the car and closed the car door ever so gently, hoping that no one could hear them as they moved away from the car.

Miranda whispered, "Let's get goin' now. The party will be over by the time we get there if we don't hurry up. I don't want to miss any more of the fun."

"I don't even care about going to the party now," said Willie. "I just want to go there to be near mama and daddy over there or at home safe and sound.

I'm really tempted to tell them everything anyway, 'cause I don't like keeping secrets from them."

"You can say that again, Willie. This is just too crazy, the four of us, out here and all alone."

Miranda raised her voice.

"You can't tell them anything y'all. You'll spoil everything."

Rae Ann then glanced all around, very slowly. "I think if we talk, we should only whisper. We don't want to attract any attention. We'll have to discuss that subject later. I guess we need to start walkin' and try not to make any noise."

"That's right 'cause we don't have a car now and we're in the dark. We're just kids, and we're in the woods, probably in the path of the *Dirt Man* and the big ol' bats. Rae Ann and me are goin' to be in so much trouble when mama and daddy find out. That is, if we live that long."

"Willie, stop talkin' like that. I already told you that nothing's going to happen," said Miranda.

"I do think we ought to walk fast. The sooner we get to the house, the better it will be for us."

So they started walking down the dirt road together when all of a sudden, they heard someone's voice.

Willie raised his eyebrows as he said "I told y'all that I heard whispers back there. You didn't believe me did you, Miranda?"

"Well, I know that I'm not goin' to answer that question, Willie."

Mary Beth said, "That don't sound like anybody that we know, does it Miranda?"

"No," said Miranda. "I think we better get ready to run, if we hear that voice again. What do you think?"

"I think you're right."

Then they did hear it again, and it sounded as if it was getting closer.

"Y'all hold on to each other's hands tight now, and make a run for it on the count of three," whispered Miranda.

"One . . . . two . . . three! Now run for your lives!"

They ran in the direction of the house, where the party was, but for some reason, they didn't run quite fast enough because up ahead about a quarter of a mile, they heard that same voice again.

Then they heard footsteps! They heard those dreaded footsteps and the raspy, overbearing, voice a few more times, so they kept running in hopes of finding some place that was safe enough to hide. No matter how far or how fast they ran, the footsteps and the voice seemed to keep up with them.

"I'm scared!" shouted Willie. "I think he's got a car or something."

"Me too, so we know we ain't staying here, so please don't stop runnin' now Willie!" shouted Rae Ann. "Come on with me Willie! We'll meet y'all back at Willie's home, Miranda. We ain't goin' to any party tonight. The *Dirt Man* or whoever or whatever it is, is probably waiting for us up ahead." Then she turned around, while holding her cousin Willie's hand, and ran in the opposite direction of where the party was.

"I'm really scared, Rae Ann. I don't want to be here. What are we goin' to do?"

"Just hold on Willie. We'll get back to the house. Don't think about being scared. Just think about what we need to do."

"I hear something again," said Willie. I think we need to hide behind those bushes over there. Maybe we can duck down and crawl to 'em or something."

The harsh sounds, the whispers, and the very distinct, daunting voice, echoed in their minds. The foul smell of the unseen critters and the thought of them scurrying around nearby put them in a state of misery.

"Yeah, I hear something too, but I believe it's coming from another direction farther down, so I don't think we need to hide behind those bushes quite yet. I think we're okay so far, but don't stop running yet. We're going to get tired, but we have to keep pushin' on."

"Okay, I'll be all right now, I guess, but I can't stop shaking." said Willie.

The dither they were in and their young age combined, made it difficult for them to make good decisions. The only thing they really knew was to continue running. After a few minutes, something in the distance caught Willie's eye.

"I see something. Hey, there's a car over there. Is somebody in it?"

"I don't know, but we don't have time to find out."

"But Rae Ann, it looks like a teenage boy in that car. What if we know that boy? What if it's Sammy?"

"Well, I guess we're far from him now 'cause I don't hear his voice. We'll walk a little bit closer to the car and see who's in there."

"Hey you, over there—don't go back there in the woods! Somebody or something's back there! Hey, is that you Sammy? If it's you, you need to turn your car around and drive on the open road to the party 'cause that's where Miranda and Mary Beth are headed. But we'd be grateful if you give me and Rae Ann a ride to my house first."

There was no answer. Then Rae Ann said, "Well, he's not talkin' to us, so there's nothin' more that we can say. We better go now Willie."

Willie turned around and looked at the teenage boy again. Then he said, "He didn't start the car up, Rae Ann."

"I know Willie. I noticed that too. Something's really wrong about that."

"Maybe we should walk closer to him. Maybe he didn't hear us."

"Willie, I'm not walkin' over there. You go ahead if you want to and I'll stay here and keep watch."

"Okay, maybe he'll drive us home or if he's hurt, maybe we can drive him to the hospital," said Willie.

"We can't drive to the hospital. We're only ten years old."

"Well, you've heard that saying, "Desperate times sometimes call for desperate measures and I'm desperate as hell in this time of need."

"Willie, you're not thinking straight cous'. Even if we were old enough to drive, we can't. We don't know how to drive good enough. We'd probably have a car accident."

"Well, that boy better be all right then."

He crept closer to the car quietly and carefully, while trying not to make a sound; but, with the kind of personality that Willie had, the silence broke when he said, "Hey Rae Ann, this dirt is mushy over here. It doesn't feel like mud. It's kinda red too. Maybe it's red clay. We learned about red clay in school just the other day for geography. I've never seen red clay in the woods before, though. Some of it is thick and darker red and slippery too. Maybe it ain't clay. Maybe it's paint mixed with dirt—but I don't see any paint cans. Oh dern! Some of it got on my good Sunday shoes. I don't know how I'm goin' to explain it to mama and daddy. Well, it's too late now."

Willie walked closer to the car, and leaned toward the teenage boy and said, "I don't see any keys and he hasn't moved a muscle. Don't this boy ever get a tan? He's ghost white. He looks like he's cold, but he's not shaking. He doesn't look right Rae Ann. Maybe he just passed out from drinkin' too much. Boy, he's goin' to be in trouble when he gets home if that's what he was doin'! I see some red color on the car seat. Uh oh! That's blood. Okay, I'm comin' back now Rae Ann."

Willie started to tremble even more than before, and he turned around and hurried back to where Rae Ann was standing.

"We need to call for help, Rae Ann," said Willie, as his words stammered from his mouth.

"We will call an ambulance Willie, but we need to go now, so please come on. Run faster than you've ever run before. I know he's hurt and he might be dead. I think the *Dirt Man* did it. I bet you already thought the same thing—and I think he'll be back here."

Then they heard the whisper again. It was a raspy voice and as it got closer, they were able to tell that it was a boy's or a man's voice. He spoke very slowly, but they still couldn't hear what was being said.

Willie said, "Uhhh . . . I hear it again Rae Ann! Do you hear it? I don't recognize it. I wish I knew who it could be. What if he jumps out at us? I'm tellin' you that I'm scared to death! I want to go home! Why did we ever go along with Miranda's stupid idea?"

"Let's get movin' Willie."

They ran as quickly as they could and Rae Ann managed to utter a few words to Willie in response to his question.

"Willie, we didn't know that Miranda and Mary Beth were planning to go through the woods until it was too late for us to do anything about it. She wasn't goin' to pay any attention to what we said. She already made up her mind. We can't think about that now, Willie. We don't have far to go now. You said the keys weren't in the ignition right?"

"Yeah, that's what I said. I hope the *Dirt Man* don't have the keys. Do you hear a car coming now?"

"No."

"Me either. I think it was my imagination. At least, I hope it was. He'd only be able to use the keys in that car anyway. Boy, I sure hope he don't come back here right now. Do you think he's following us? Maybe I should look back. We need to know what he looks like."

"Well, he could be following us, but don't look back. Just keep running. If you look back, it'll just make you more afraid than you are now. Besides, he might really come after us if he knows that we can identify him. He'd probably try twice as hard to get us then. I don't want to take that chance little Willie boy."

"I don't guess that I do either Rae Ann, but I'm not feelin' good about any of this. We might be doomed. I hope he don't find us and kill us."

Rae Ann and Willie looked at each other, feeling alarmed and held each other's hands again and fled for their lives once more. Poor young Willie was frantic and his knees shook, and he got so tired that he started to wobble, but at a slower pace, he continued running, until he tripped over something. Rae Ann grabbed his arm and pulled him up to keep him from falling. He managed to compose himself, get back on both feet. It felt as though they were running endlessly. They both shook like leaves engulfed in a strong wind. Tears poured out of their eyes and rolled down their faces, and their mouths were opened from fright and horror. They were so very tired and almost out of breath, as they heaved when they inhaled.

"I'm never going to do anything like this again," said Rae Ann.

"I'm not either," said Willie. We should have known better. I don't ever want to go out with Miranda or with Mary Beth again."

"You said it cousin! I feel the same way!"

"You just leave it to me, Rae Ann. Mama and daddy probably won't let them near us for a long time."

Willie finally spotted the porch lights at home up ahead, but that didn't keep them from running even then 'cause anything could happen—even within a minute. Enormous relief was what they felt once they got to the door. They were thankful to get there safely.

CHAPTER 4

With rapid motion, Willie opened the door and they hurried inside, locked all the doors and the windows, and walked their shaky little bodies toward the couch, still holding hands, clinching them tightly, until they stopped suddenly, in the middle of the room, and looked at each other. At that moment, they both burst into tears again.

Rae Ann and Willie realized that something was terribly wrong.

She whispered, "Willie? The door was unlocked before we got here."

"It sure was. I wonder if Miranda even locked the door before we left tonight."

"I tell you what Willie . . . let's grab something for protection."

Willie said, "That's a good idea 'cause we can hit him upside the head if he tries to lay his hands on us."

They froze where they stood and started to look all around them.

"I've got something right here, Rae Ann. If he comes near us, I'll hit him with this piece of wood that I found by the fireplace."

"I don't see anybody or hear anything. How about you, Rae Ann?"

He didn't want to look through the windows to see if anyone was outside the window. He was afraid that the *Dirt Man* or some other scary being would look back at him with gazing eyes.

"Let's just sit here together by the wall until Miranda or your family gets back here, Willie. I wonder if Mary Beth is goin' home or comin' here."

"I don't know."

Willie sat down against the wall, beside Rae Ann.

"I've never been in this kind of situation before. This has got to be the scariest mess I've ever been in."

"Yeah . . . me too."

"This is the best place for us to sit. We can see in every direction, and nobody can sneak up behind us."

They listened for any unusual sounds as they sat.

"I sure hope those girls get back here safely tonight. They're older than we are but they're not very smart," whispered Rae Ann.

"If Miranda doesn't get back before your mama and daddy get back, I don't know what we'll do. Do you have any idea of what we're goin' to say?"

Just then, there was a loud knock on the door.

"All right Willie, what are we going to do now?"

"You know there's a peep hole in the door, Rae Ann. You have to pull yourself together, get on that floor on your hands and knees, and crawl to the door, stand up and look through the peep hole to see who it is."

"Hey, I don't think so cousin. You're the only male here right now, so you're the man of the house, so you have to do it."

"Okay, I guess I am the man of the house now, so I'll be brave and do just that."

"Well, what are you waitin' for, Willie?"

Then there was another knock, and this time it was a louder, heavier, pounding sound. They became even more frightened. They could hear the clanging of the door knocker.

Willie got down on the floor and crawled and slowly got up, leaning against the wall, in case somebody or something terrible was peering into the peep hole. Then as he stood up, he leaned over very slowly, quietly, and carefully and looked into the peep hole and to his surprise, there was Miranda. She was standing there plowing her fists into the door, screaming, shaking and crying.

He opened the door quickly and shouted, "Miranda, we're so glad you're all right."

Miranda said, "Quick Willie, close the door 'cause he might not be far behind me. What took you so long to open up the door?"

"Well, we didn't know that it was you."

Once Miranda got inside, Rae Ann jumped up and they all gave each other a big hug and then sat down.

"Miranda asked, "Don't y'all think that this kind of an odd place for us to sit?"

Rae Ann blurted, "You want to talk about odd? Don't you think it was kind of odd that you didn't lock the door to the house before we left tonight? Why didn't you lock the door Miranda? What is wrong with you?"

"Uh, I didn't lock it? I guess I didn't think it was a big deal. I'm sorry. I was wrong."

Willie gritted his teeth together and said, "Somebody could've been in the house! What if somebody was here when we got here? We could've been killed! Didn't you pay attention to any of the stories that Charles and I told y'all? We told y'all those stories for a reason. I want my house key!"

"All right. Fine. Here it is."

"Where's Mary Beth, Miranda?" asked Rae Ann.

"I don't know. We decided to fend for ourselves 'cause we were slowing each other down when we ran. We decided to meet each other back here after the party. I'm not sure which way she went. I have to say though—I did see someone nearby and I know it wasn't her. I didn't get a good, clear look at him, but I know it was a big boy or a man. I didn't look back. I just kept runnin' until I got here. So no one else has knocked or tried to get inside?" asked Miranda.

"No, as far as we know, nobody has come here at all. Do you think she got out of the woods?" asked Rae Ann.

"I sure hope so. She did say that she might go home instead. I'll call her shortly so we can find out if that's where she went or maybe Sammy finally showed up and she's with him."

"We don't think that's likely Miranda. We saw a car with a teenage boy in it. What color is Sammy's car?" asked Rae Ann.

"It's blue. It's a blue El Camino," answered Miranda.

"Well, the car was an El Camino, but she wasn't in the car with him when we were there. We tried to talk to him, but maybe he just didn't want to talk to us, 'cause he was scared like us or maybe he didn't hear me talkin' to him because he was too drunk and he was sleepin', except that wouldn't explain why there was blood on the car seat. Maybe he got in a fight. I don't know why he didn't answer me," said Willie.

Miranda frowned and then started to cry again. "Sammy doesn't drink and he never gets into fights. I hope he's all right. He's a nice guy. I hope Mary Beth is all right, too. She's my best friend. I don't know what I'd do without her. What color hair did the boy that y'all saw have? Could he still be there? Maybe we can go back together."

"He had blonde hair and he was there then, but we don't know if he's there now. We ain't about to go back there. Have you lost your dern mind Miranda? The *Dirt Man* knows we were in the woods and he might be here in our neighborhood now. You even said he might have been behind you. What if he's outside waiting for us? He's probably already done something with Sammy. Do you want us to die too?"

"NO!"

"Well, we'll call an ambulance and the police will go there, so don't you think for a minute that we're going back there."

Just as Willie started to walk towards the phone, Miranda cringed and said, "Willie, what's on your shoes? There's something on the floor too. You're making footprints with your shoes."

Willie stopped walking and took off his shoes and said, "Hey, it's that stuff that I walked in when we were in the woods. I knew that couldn't be red clay. It looks redder in here than it did in the woods. Oh no . . . It looks like blood. That's twice now, that I've seen blood."

"I'm goin' to call for an ambulance now," said Willie.

He made the anonymous call and then went back to where he had been sitting.

"We better see how much of it got on the floor so we can clean it up," said Rae Ann.

"Fine, but you don't have to be so bossy. Remember I'm older than you are," said Miranda.

"Yeah that's true, but when have you ever acted like it?" asked Rae Ann sarcastically.

"You sure didn't act like it tonight."

Willie thought that he should say something.

"All right, that's enough. This kind of talk ain't helping anything at all, even though Rae Ann's right."

"Miranda and I can get the blood off the floor, but not off my shoes. We might need them for evidence."

"That is a good point," said Rae Ann.

After they completed that task, Willie put his shoes in the closet. About fifteen minutes passed and Miranda decided to call Mary Beth. The answering machine was on.

"Well, this isn't a good sign. Nobody answered the phone. I'm going to call again and leave a message this time."

So Miranda dialed the number again, leaving a message for Mary Beth to call her at Willie's home or at her home just as soon as she got her message. Mary Beth's parents had gone to the party too, so she knew they wouldn't be home for a while.

CHAPTER 5

They sat back down, together, still fearing the worst would happen if they sat too close to the doors or too near the windows. They sat there for almost three hours and then finally, they could hear Russ at the door and they jumped up and ran to the door. They were so happy and so relieved to see him and Maggie come in that they put their arms around them, and then Willie exclaimed, "We just love y'all to pieces daddy!"

Miranda even had her arms around them.

"We love y'all too, but what's this all about Willie?" asked his daddy, Russ.

"Willie, you look frail and a little shook up. Are you coming down with a cold Willie?"

"Mama, I think you might be right. I don't feel good at all. If something real serious is wrong, I just wanted to let y'all know how much I love you."

"Hmm," grunted his daddy.

"What I want to know is if you gave these children anything to eat tonight, Miranda?" asked Maggie.

"Well, we got so busy, doin' things 'n' all, that there just wasn't time for us to eat anything. Then with all the stuff we were doin', time just slipped away from us. I asked them if they were sleepy, but they told me that they weren't sleepy at all," replied Miranda. Miranda continued showing that she was devious, even after this terrible experience.

"Six hours didn't allow y'all enough time to eat anything or to remember that there's a bedtime for these children? Now, you know Willie likes to get into the snacks the minute we walk out the door. You told me so yourself. I don't see one open bag of snacks. Why aren't they tired? It's almost 4 o'clock in the morning."

"Yeah, something isn't quite adding up with your explanation Miranda. Your answers don't hold the *weight of beans* to me. You better come up with something better than that, to expect for us to believe it."

"You're right, daddy. Miranda's not a good babysitter, and she shouldn't stay with us when you and mama go out. Mary Beth shouldn't either, since she's Miranda's best friend. She'd treat us the same way."

"Okay, Miranda, we're going to pay you for staying with Willie and Rae Ann tonight, but I'm afraid you've messed up, so we won't be calling you again anytime soon. Do you hear me? You know you're still like family to us though, and you're still welcome here anytime as long as Maggie or I'm here," said Russ.

While sniffing, Miranda said, "I'm sorry Mr. and Mrs. Matthews, and Willie, and Rae Ann. I'm especially sorry that I ruined the time that you two spent with me tonight."

"Oh, don't cry Miranda. You're still like family to us, just like daddy said." Then he looked at his mama and daddy with his big brown eyes, as innocently as he could.

"Okay Miranda, you can get your sweater now and I'll drive you home," said Russ.

Then he moved his head about and breathed in some air. "Ugh" . . . he said as he crinkled his nose and clinched his lips close together when he smelled something foul.

"It's a little stuffy in here and it smells in here. Maybe I should open up a window."

Willie didn't want to tell his mama or daddy how afraid he was or why—not yet anyway.

"Daddy, please don't. I feel sick and I'll catch my death of cold. Miranda might have stepped in something before she got here tonight. I think she put on some kind of stale perfume to kill the odor, but now it smells worse."

"Mr. Matthews, I did buy some new perfume and when I sprayed it on my wrists, I realized it was the wrong bottle of perfume, but let me assure you that the smell isn't from something that I stepped in! Maybe Little Willie stepped in something. Ain't that right, Willie?"

"Uh, well, I couldn't have stepped in anything inside the house."

"All right now, you two stop right now! I'm going to keep the windows closed. Let me get you home right now, Miranda."

"Thank you, Mr. Matthews. You have no idea how much I appreciate that, but first, may I talk to Willie and Rae Ann alone for a minute? I'd like to tell them goodnight." said Miranda.

"Sure you can. I'll wait for you in the car."

"Well, I'm going into the kitchen and fix some chicken noodle soup for these two," said Maggie.

Miranda looked sharply at Willie. "You sure know how to pour it on! I must have stepped in something? Couldn't you have come up with something better than that to tell them?"

"I didn't have time to think about it. You know everything about this whole night stinks. Why didn't you let us stay here with you like you were supposed to? We could have had a good time right here."

"A good time doin' what, little Willie? I would've been bored to death."

"What's wrong with you, girl? Look at the mess you got us into. It wasn't worth it. Wouldn't you rather stay here and be bored, especially after what happened tonight? What we did was stupid. We could have been killed."

Then she looked at Willie and looked at Rae Ann and said, "I'm surprised you didn't tell on me."

Rae Ann said, "We wanted to, but after talkin' about it, we decided not to yet. We saved your hind end from getting into trouble only because we would have been dragged into it, right along with you."

"Since when, do the two of you make decisions about me? Oh, don't even bother tellin' me 'cause at least we can say we're even now."

"You'll never learn will you, Miranda?" asked Willie. It's sad that Rae Ann and me, who are years younger than you, are more grown up than you are."

"Well, I won't comment on that remark, Willie, so good night," said Miranda. Then she walked out the door.

CHAPTER 6

When she got into the car she asked, "Can we stop at Mary Beth's house, Mr. Matthews? I just want to make sure that she's all right since she's home alone."

"Sure, we'll definitely do that." Then they drove towards Mary Beth's house.

"It sure is dark out here. I hate to think that anybody would walk out here alone. Anything could happen," said Miranda.

"Yep, it would be really foolish for anyone to be out here alone. That's why we don't think that any of you kids should be out here—gallivanting around out here. It's gotten dangerous," said Russ.

Russ pulled up into their driveway and waited for Miranda while she went to check on Mary Beth in hopes of finding her there. She rang the doorbell. It was no use! She still wasn't there. She wondered where Mary Beth could be. She almost did the decent thing and told the truth, but being self-centered and stubborn which she sometimes was, she kept what she knew to herself. She had no intentions of telling anyone anything at all about Mary Beth being with her and the Matthews' children out in the woods. They'd have to practically pry that secret from her. Miranda came back to the car.

"Mary Beth is probably sleeping or maybe she decided to go out. She should have called me though."

Russ didn't think that what Miranda said was peculiar since Mary Beth was a typical eighteen year old.

"Miranda, now listen to me. She's probably hangin' around with some friends and she forgot to call. Her parents were still at the party when Maggie and I left. They were really enjoyin' themselves but I'm sure they'll be home soon. I better get you home now. I know your family is there. They left the party an hour or so before we did."

"Okay, Mr. Matthews," answered Miranda. She didn't want to tell him how worried she really was. She continued with her dishonesty—her little deceptive act, during the ride to her home.

On the road towards Miranda's home, Miranda shouted, "Do you see something? Is there someone beside the road? Maybe it's an animal, Mr. Matthews."

"No, I don't think so Miranda. I'll stop the car and take a look if you'd like, though."

"No sir. There's no need for that."

"Who or what did it look like?"

"Maybe a man or a big boy. I could be wrong. Maybe it was just a wild animal."

"Yeah, it could have been. You sound scared. What are you afraid of Miranda? I won't let anything happen to you."

"Uh, I don't know. Maybe a bat swooped down by the road."

"Don't worry, Miranda. I don't think it's a bat."

"Well, I'll always be afraid of those."

"You kids have heard a lot of bat stories, but remember that some of them are just myths."

"Yeah, I know, but they still scare me."

Then they arrived at Miranda's home.

"Mr. Matthews? Can you stay out here in the car until I get into the house?"

"Don't worry 'cause that's what I intend to do."

So she walked to her door and checked on the window sill for the house key, which was usually hidden in the corner, and was relieved when it was there, feeling that it was safe to unlock the door and go inside. She then waved and went inside. He waved back to her and waited a few minutes before starting his drive home.

Miranda looked out the window after turning lights on and waved again. Then he pulled out the driveway and about a half mile down the road, he saw something. He drove very slowly. Then he saw a large, vicious bear, and heard it snarling as it picked up remnants of meat which had laid dormant, gnawing at the meat and ripping its teeth into it with great force. It guarded its meal, as its eyes, moving from left to right, scoped the vast darkness, listening for sounds from anyone or anything that dared to try to take its feast away. It couldn't have been scraps that the bear pulled out of trash cans. Russ wanted to do something, but he knew he didn't have his rifle in the car, so he kept driving.

When he arrived home, he said to his wife Maggie, "That girl acted a little peculiar the entire way home. She was right about one thing though. She thought she saw something walkin' along the side of the road and I think what she saw was a bear. Maggie, on my way home from Miranda's I saw a bear and it was scoffing—downed a huge piece of meat. That bear was chompin' it down like there's no tomorrow. Woo! I mean to tell you, I'm damn glad that I wasn't its prey! It's goin' to have a full belly tonight! I don't know what kind of animal it found, but it had to have been a big one. I've never seen a bear scarf down that much raw meat all at once! I know it wasn't a deer." Then he shook his head. He was awe struck by what he saw by the road.

Maggie said, "Well, did you shoot it?"

"Naw, I didn't have my rifle with me."

"You're not goin' out there to shoot it now are you?"

"Nope. It's probably gone by now. It probably gone to sleep somewhere and that's what I'm goin' to do. I'll make a call when I get up in a couple of hours. Someone will go there and check things out."

"Okay then, I wanted to talk to you about the children. I think something funny's going on and I don't mean in a humorous way either Russ. They're so jumpy. Every time they heard a noise, they *just about jumped out of their skin*. I don't know what in the world happened tonight, but I don't like it one little bit. You go ahead and get some sleep now though. I think I'll go to bed now too."

"That's right, we'll talk after we get some shut eye."

"Yeah Russ, it's been a long day."

Willie and Rae Ann tossed and turned in their beds that night. Both of them woke up numerous times. Willie was in his bedroom. He held a stuffed bear tightly. He hadn't held it at all for years. Tonight, was different though. It was comforting for him to hold it. It kept him from feeling alone. He reminded himself that his parents were in the next room and when he thought about that, he felt more at ease and finally got a little sleep.

In Dawn's colorful room, Rae Ann already had her own stuffed animal with her, but she cuddled with Dawn's stuffed animals too. She placed them all around her. Then she found some paper and a pencil, too, and started jotting down words that described what she was feeling. She turned her words into a poem and even completed it. Although it was difficult for her to sleep, concentrating on the poem helped her to forget the agonizing fear she felt that evening. She soon drifted off to sleep.

How could so many things happen in one night?

The next morning, Willie and Rae Ann decided to call Mary Beth. They were still worried about her. Miranda didn't call to let them know if she'd heard from her or not and Mary Beth didn't call. Maybe she's sleeping. If anything was wrong, her parents would have called to find out if anyone had seen or heard from her.

"We'll wait until your parents go outside and then we can call," said Rae Ann.

"That sounds good, cousin."

"Okay, Rae Ann, they've gone out to the garden, so we can call now," said Willie.

They called, but no one answered the phone. Then they decided to wait before calling again.

Then Willie told Rae Ann that he was going to go outside to help his mama and daddy in the garden. He didn't feel afraid since it was daylight and since his parents were there. Rae Ann decided that she'd help too.

When Willie opened the door, he could hear them talking, but he couldn't hear clearly what was being said because they were speaking in very soft voices. As a matter-of-fact, when Willie and Rae Ann started to walk out the door, his daddy told them to go back inside because they were having a private discussion about something very important.

Russ soon went back inside the house and told Willie and Rae Ann to stay inside the house until they were told to do otherwise.

"Is something wrong daddy?" asked Willie.

"I'm not sure, but I can't talk about right now anyway son. Your mama will be inside in a minute and then I'm going out, so you and Rae Ann stay in here just like I told you. I might bring home some snacks or a hamburger for y'all, so behave yourself, Willie."

"I will daddy."

"You be good for your grandma and for your granddaddy too, girl."

"I sure will, Uncle Russ."

"Daddy wouldn't talk about bringing us anything back if he knew we went out last night, so I guess we're not in any trouble, Rae Ann," said Willie. "I wonder why Charles, Francis, and Dawn don't have to come home."

"I guess he thinks they're all right wherever they are right now," replied Rae Ann. "Your mama and daddy probably know exactly where they are."

"I know I don't want to go outside without mama or daddy there anyway 'cause we might be in danger."

"I think all of us cousins need to get together and have a meeting tonight, don't you Rae Ann? We need to find out if anybody's heard anything about what's been goin' on around here."

"Yes, I do. I'll start roundin' everybody up that I can. You're going to have to talk to your mama and daddy about having everybody over here," said Rae Ann.

"I can do that," replied Willie. Usually, if something serious is going on, everybody gets together to talk things out."

Rae Ann started making the phone calls and learned that their young cousins, brothers, sisters, and friends couldn't go anywhere either.

Rae Ann walked over to Willie and told him that she just spoke to Junior and he said that everyone's families were going to meet at Town Hall.

"Dern, then we can't see any of our cousins tonight. You know when meetings are held at Town Hall, something big is goin' on."

"I wonder if they saw the Dirt Man. Maybe they arrested him. I'd be glad then."

"You and me both," said Willie. "I still think we need to have our own meeting, maybe tomorrow night, after we find out why they had one."

"Yeah," replied Rae Ann.

"I hear a car in the driveway," said Willie. "Let's go see what daddy brought home for us. I wonder what he's goin' to tell us."

Willie and Rae Ann were so young and naive. They assumed that Mary Beth must have gotten home safely since they weren't told anything differently. They thought for sure that something would have been said about it by now if anything terrible had happened. Little, did they know . . .

Russ opened the door and called Willie and Rae Ann into the living room. He said, "Hey children, here's your food."

As they walked into the kitchen, Willie asked, "Hey what's the special occasion daddy?"

"There's nothing special going on today son. I thought I'd get y'all something that you'd enjoy eating before I talk to you two. So go ahead and eat and then we three will have a serious discussion."

"Okay daddy," answered Willie.

"Okay, Uncle Russ and thanks for the good eats," replied Rae Ann.

"What do you think he wants to talk to us about, Willie?"

"Well, I suspect that they found something out about the *Dirt Man*, Rae Ann."

They both ate as quickly as they could and then Russ walked into the kitchen and sat down with them.

"Okay, do either one of you know a teenage boy named Sammy Johnson?"

"We heard of a boy named Sammy. We're not quite sure what his last name is," replied Willie.

Willie then went on to add, "We heard that he's Mary Beth's boyfriend, but we don't know him."

"Well, I have to tell y'all something that's pretty sad because I feel that you need to know. Maybe it'll help the two of you to be careful and let us know if you see anything or anyone suspicious looking."

"What is it Uncle Russ?" asked Rae Ann.

"The police found a blue-colored El Camino at the entrance of the woods this morning. It might be Mary Beth's boyfriend's car, but they haven't seen her or Sammy. We're not sure if he and Mary Beth left the car and walked somewhere or if they left in another car. The police haven't even told us yet if it's his car for sure. They won't tell us what the numbers are on the license plates. I guess they have to keep most everything confidential until they get all their facts together. Y'all know she's eighteen now. We hope they didn't get married. We know that Sammy's on the fast track with girls. He doesn't work, he doesn't get along with his parents, and he just doesn't do much of anything. At least we know that he doesn't drink or smoke or get into fights, though. We do know that Mary Beth and him planned to see each other. We found that out from Miranda. Miranda sure has turned into a disappointment. She used to be such a nice girl. But anyway, it could also be possible that Mary Beth never met up with Sammy, and went home instead, and then went somewhere with her parents because we haven't seen or heard from them either—not since the party anyway. I know you've been wonderin' where Charles, Dawn, and Francis have been. We feel that it's best if the other children stay wherever they were last night. We have already discussed it and we all agree that it's for the best. We just don't want any children wanderin' around in the neighborhood right now. We'll go get your brother and sisters when the police feel it's safe enough."

"That's fine daddy. Daddy, usually when something bad happens, all our relatives get together here at our house for a meeting. Can we have our meeting this weekend?" Willie asked.

"Well, if we do, it'll have to be tomorrow night. It might be good for all of us to be together anyway," said Russ. "I'll discuss it with the others tonight before the town meeting begins."

Then Russ left the room and Willie said to Rae Ann, "There isn't any important reason for us to tell daddy yet is there Rae Ann? I know if Sammy got killed last night, we're going to have to tell him and mama everything, but he didn't say that anybody died, so we don't need to say anything yet. Do you agree with me?"

"Yep, I sure do Willie." Rae Ann hoped in her mind that they hadn't let things go too far. She knew that her grandma and granddaddy would be really upset with her for keeping these kinds of secrets. Then after careful thought she said, "Willie, maybe we should start thinking about telling everything that we know very soon."

"Yeah, I was just thinking the same thing. We'll have to accept whatever punishment they give us, but do you mind if we wait until after our meeting tomorrow? If they tell us that we can't have our meeting tomorrow, we'll tell them everything after they get home from their town meeting tonight."

"It'll feel good to do the right thing, Willie." said Rae Ann.

"Yeah, it does. Now, I've got some things to do, and I think mama wants you to help her with something."

Willie and Rae Ann forgot their troubles for a few hours.

CHAPTER 7

Russ's sister, Millie, stayed with Willie and Rae Ann that evening instead of attending the town meeting. She knew her husband would fill her in on the discussion of the night, and share any new information with her concerning the recent murders in the town.

So Russ, Maggie, and Millie's husband, named Warren, left and headed to town, to attend the meeting together. Willie's mama and daddy first spoke to their relatives before the meeting began and they decided to meet at Russ's home the next day.

The meeting began, and the mood turned somber within the first few minutes. The chairman took care of his usual business, but then he frowned and paused for a moment. Things had taken a turn for the worse. He had the burden of sharing some horrible news to the community. He informed everyone that some bodies were found and that the decayed bodies had been there for quite some time and were unrecognizable, so they couldn't be identified for now. Because of their condition, it could take months to identify them. Two more bodies found were murdered during the past day or two. No one knew who those two victims were yet either, but once they had that information, their families would be the first ones to be told. Everyone was reminded to stay out of the wooded areas. They were also informed about animals dominating the area and that one or more victims may have been attacked by a bear, or some other vicious animal, and eaten.

"Maggie? I wonder if that dern bear that I saw, was eatin' a person. What if it was someone we know?"

"Oh, my heavens Russ. I sure hope not," said Maggie.

"I should have gone home and grabbed my rifle and shot the son-of-a-bitch."

"Well, don't let it bother you now, Russ."

Families were urged to go straight home after the meeting and to lock all their doors and to keep their windows closed and locked too. If any of them owned guns or rifles, they needed to keep them locked up, but within reach and to make sure if they were going to use them, that they followed the gun laws to the letter. He urged for the townsfolk to beware and take precaution if they were approached by any strangers and to check their vehicles first, look through their car windows before entering inside and if the vehicles were locked, to make sure they were still locked before opening their car doors, just so they'd know that no one was hiding inside them. They were also urged to call the authorities if anything appeared to be different about their vehicles. Once they arrive at their homes, they were again, asked to call the authorities if anything appeared different and to keep their children inside until further notice. The chairman also suggested that no one walk alone anywhere until further notice.

Then he decided to adjourn the meeting early because he felt it was unwise for any of them to be out late with a ruthless killer on the loose. Luckily, everyone was parked near one another. The desperation, the despair, and sorrow was apparent, with each one wondering who the victims were that had fallen prey to undeniably, some of the worst, heinous acts of violence. The dominance of this killer was felt by everyone. Russ and Maggie shuddered at the thought of one of their own loved ones dying.

At home, Willie and Rae Ann continued to stay near each other. They were almost inseparable. Millie also noticed that they were acting a little odd.

When Maggie, Russ and Warren walked in the door, Willie and Rae Ann ran up to them and hugged them again, the same way they did the previous night. Millie looked down at them fondly, but was a little concerned about their actions. Then she asked, "Are you two all right?"

"We're fine, Aunt Millie."

Their Aunt Millie said, "I know those two aren't usually this cuddly. When y'all were out tonight, they followed me into every room that I walked into. Every time they heard a little noise, they jumped a mile high. They're acting like they're scared of something."

"We know what you mean Millie," said Maggie. They acted the same way last night. I'm not positive, but I think something might have happened between Miranda and them. It wouldn't explain why Miranda hugged us when we walked in the door though. Whatever it is, Russ is determined to get to the bottom of it, so we'll know what's goin' on with the children pretty soon."

"Don't y'all worry about us mama," said Willie. "Rae Ann and I are just fine. We just want y'all to know that we don't want to be away from y'all—not even for a second."

"Lucky for the two of you, we don't have time to have any long discussions tonight because it's late, so we'll talk tomorrow about this new found touchy-feely kind of love you two have for all of us all of a sudden."

"Yeah, I think it's time for you two to go to your rooms and get some sleep," said Maggie. I'll come and check on y'all in a minute or two. Now tell everyone goodnight."

Then Willie and Rae Ann said goodnight, Willie first wanted to find out what was said at the meeting and if the family was going to have their own meeting the next day. "Daddy, is there any news about Sammy and have you made a decision about us having a family meeting tomorrow?"

Russ answered, "No son, there's no new news about Sammy and yes, we are going to have our own meeting here at home tomorrow."

"I knew you'd do the right thing, daddy."

"Okay, get to bed now." Then Willie and Rae Ann went to their rooms.

As soon as the children left the living room, Russ suggested that his sister and his brother-in-law stay in their home for the night. It took very little persuasion to get the couple to stay, as they were feeling a little uneasy about going out after the discussion at the town meeting.

"We sure do appreciate your invitation to spend the night here Russ. You didn't have to ask twice. The things that we learned tonight have put the whole community on edge. This is really scary man. This is something that has even grown men like us shakin' in our boots."

"You're right about that. You two can stay here as long as you need to."

"I'm glad we're havin' our meeting tomorrow. Little Willie is looking forward to it, too."

"Well, I think my son has been up to something, but he's counting on this meeting. I don't want any surprises from him, Rae Ann, or Miranda though. I think they'll come around and see things in a different way tomorrow and let us know what they've been hiding from us. I think tomorrow will be a good time for us all to get together and to try to take care of a lot of issues."

"Yeah Russ, I know your boy will do the right thing, just as he knew you would," Millie softly giggled as she thought about her nephew's comments to Russ about doin' the right thing.

"Your son has stamped his own seal-of-approval as far as you doin' the right thing. He really wants to have that meeting don't he?"

"All right, sis," said Russ, "you can stop your goofy humor anytime now, or we're going to have to send you to your room. Are you hiding anything from us? Exactly what went on here tonight?"

"Not a thing Russ. Seriously, you know how much Willie looks up to you. It's a good thing."

"Yep sis. I know he does. He's a good son. I think he's going to grow up to be a fine young man, too."

Then they all talked about their children; for a few brief moments, everything seemed just as normal as ever, the way it used to be—without having to worry about killers and kidnappers or other criminals or fears that seemed to take over their community.

Willie and Rae Ann were still very afraid that the murderer was after them, so in their cozy beds, they tossed and turned again, thinking that they would be taken away if they slept. Finally, neither one of the two could fight their tiredness any longer and drifted off for a few hours; finding themselves still safe and sound the next morning.

CHAPTER 8

After breakfast, they all waited patiently for the other relatives to get there. While they waited, the phone rang and Russ answered it. He was only on the phone for a moment. After he hung up, he smiled and shouted with the sound of satisfaction, "Hot damn! Mary Beth's parents are home now. They decided to stay at the Tallhouse family's home after the party. They weren't able to drive anywhere after the party 'cause they had a little too much to drink. That doesn't explain why no one's seen them since then, though. Russ decided that they must have had something important to take care of. He hoped that Mary Beth was with them by now."

"I wonder if they've spoken with Miranda yet," said Warren.

"I don't know. Maybe we should ask Miranda and her family to come too."

"That's a good idea, honey."

Willie stood in the doorway and listened to the conversation.

"Miranda's comin' daddy?" asked Willie.

"Yeah, we have some good reasons to invite her parents here today, son. They need to know how Miranda's been acting lately and if she's seen Mary Beth."

Willie found himself at a loss of words. Then he shrugged his shoulders, sighed and said, "Whatever you say, daddy." He knew that the truth could come out that day, but he really felt the same way his daddy did and he was prepared to tell the truth, too. His conscience bothered him and he didn't want to hide what he knew or what he did much longer. It was time for the whole truth to be told.

"It's important for them to keep an eye on that girl, Willie boy."

"You're right about that, daddy."

"Okay Willie, they'll all be here soon. Are you all right Willie?" asked Russ.

"I sure am, daddy."

"Are you and your cousins planning to go outside in the backyard? I'm asking because we were told at Town Hall to keep our children inside, so I think it would be best for y'all to stay inside today."

Willie was disappointed and said, "But daddy, what room are we going to have our meeting in?"

Then the doorbell rang.

Russ said, "Ah, Willie, answer the door and I'll think about it and let you know in a couple of minutes. Then Russ stepped outside. When he came back in, he called Willie to the living room and said, "There are no cars in the garage or anything in there that can hurt y'all, and since it's attached to the house, it should fine for y'all to hold your meeting in there. I don't want any of y'all to go in or out of the other door for any reason. Only use the door that leads to the den. There's a window on it, too."

"Yeah, and the little curtain is still hangin' on it in case we want our privacy. We need some chairs, too. We need some because we'll probably be in there for a couple of hours or longer. We have a lot of things to discuss."

"There are four chairs in the corner and you can sit on the steps if you want to. Leave the curtain open so we can check on y'all. Willie, we still need to have a talk about you being so jumpy lately. Let's plan on having that discussion today."

"Yeah, we'll plan on it daddy, and I'll be sure to tell Rae Ann."

The doorbell rang and almost everyone was there.

"Okay y'all! We'll start our meeting soon. Maggie fixed some food for everyone, so just help yourselves. It's in the kitchen," said Russ. "The children can go to the garage for their meeting. They'll use the door that divides the house and the garage. We'll be able to keep an eye on them."

Willie and some of the others came into the room and Willie said, "We just want to let y'all know that we're going to start the meeting soon. I want to wait for a few more minutes 'cause Lori's not here yet with Aunt Edna and Uncle James. Where's Mary Beth? Miranda's not here with her parents yet either."

"We haven't heard from Aunt Edna or Uncle James yet son," said Russ. "Remember, we don't want any of y'all outdoors without an adult today, especially after it turns dark out there. Y'all know that the giant bats might get you," Russ said as he moved his hand over his mouth. He tried to hide his huge smile.

Willie said, "Don't worry. We ain't going anywhere." Then the children left the room.

Maggie said, "Russ, you can get that smile off your face now. How long are we going to tell the children that ol' bat myth? Don't you think it's about time for us to tell them the truth? We need to tell them how lucky we are to have bats around here 'cause they save us money. We don't have to spend as much on pesticides, or on insecticides for the farm. Do I need to go on about it?"

"No, Maggie, please don't go on about it. We all know we need the bats, but at least we know the children won't run off anywhere at night if they think they'll carry them away. Listen now—I'll tell Willie the truth about bats real soon. I gotta tell you though, that I've really enjoyed tellin' that story, and I'm going to miss watchin' their reactions."

"Don't be so hard on the ol' boy Maggie. You can't blame him for wanting to have a little fun," said Blake.

"We have serious matters to take care of today."

Blake said, "Maggie, we can't let everything bother us. We have to try to enjoy ourselves sometimes; if we don't, we might feel like we're goin' crazy."

Maggie was just about to speak, but then the phone rang.

"I'll answer it!" exclaimed Willie, from the garage. Then he ran to the phone.

"Hello, this is the Matthews residence. Who's callin' and who would you like to talk to?"

Then he was quiet, as he listened to the caller, and said, "We're having a meeting in the garage. Okay, we will Uncle James."

Then Willie called for his daddy.

"Daddy? Uncle James is on the phone. He wants to talk to you."

"Okay, I'm coming Willie."

"You go back into the garage with your cousins and have your meeting Willie."

"All right, daddy."

Willie wondered what was bothering his Uncle James, but he didn't say anything else about it; instead, he went back inside the garage.

Rae Ann asked, "Is everything all right, Willie?"

"I'm not sure. Daddy won't tell me anything about what' going on right now, but I'm going to try to find out. Well, let's start the meeting. I'm glad we don't have to keep the door open. At least we'll have some privacy. We'll just crack it open a little bit if we need to hear what they're sayin' in the next room. Rae Ann, I'm not sure we can tell the others yet, about what we did the other night."

"Okay Willie, but I don't like it. How much longer is it going to be before we tell them what we did and what we know about Sammy and Mary Beth?"

"It ain't going to be much longer Rae Ann. I promise. I just can't tell them right now. It's too hard. How do you feel about it?"

"Well, it ain't right, but I know my grandma and granddaddy would be hurt. They'll probably be more upset if we don't tell them though. Willie boy, we'll have to tell them soon."

"We will. Everybody's supposed to go to your house next weekend."

"We'll be in a lot of trouble when they find out that we sneaked out to go to the party, so do you think we'll still all get together, even with all the killing that's been goin' on?" asked Rae Ann.

"There haven't been any reported killings out your way though, so maybe they'll take that into consideration."

"I sure hope you're right, Willie."

Willie then rounded up all of his cousins and began the meeting.

"Okay cousins, let's get this meeting started. Dawn will take the minutes of the meeting and Francis will read them back to us at our next meeting. Today's subjects are as follows:

1. **Strange happenings in the neighborhood**

2. **The *Dirt Man***

"First does anyone have anything they'd like to say before I start speaking?" After Willie waited for a few minutes, then he began.

"First, we'll take attendance. Well, for the sake of time, let's just say that everybody's here except Lori, Miranda and Mary Beth."

"Okay, now that's taken care of. You all know why we're here today. There have been some murders here in our town and in some of our surrounding areas. It's a terrible thing. If anyone knows anything or has heard anything about these murders prior to today, you can speak now. The room was silent. Then Francis spoke and said, "I have something to say, but not right now."

"Anyone else?" asked Willie.

No one answered.

"Well, okay then, we'll close that subject for this afternoon," announced Willie.

Then Miranda walked in and said "I'd like to wait to speak also."

Willie looked at her sharply and said, "So, you're finally here. I believe you're going to have a lot of talkin' to do today." Then he asked her to just find a place to sit.

"Now, the next subject is the *Dirt Man*. I would just like to start off by reminding each of you about the last time we met outdoors, and my brother Charles and me told y'all the story about that scoundrel. We just want you to beware, and for goodness sakes—stay out of the woods!"

Willie was just about to adjourn when all of a sudden; there was a loud cry in the room beside them. Willie said, "You all know from experience that we can't go in there. We have to wait till they tell us we can. If things start sounding *out-of-hand*, though, we might need to hide or somethin', I guess."

Then he paused for a moment and after giving it some thought, he said, "It's too quiet in there. I can't hear anything that they're saying, so I'm goin' over there, a little closer and open the door, and then I'll lean against the door and try to hear what they're talkin' about."

They all thought it was a good idea, so they all got up and quietly walked closer to the door near Willie so they could hear too. Willie looked at his cousins and whispered "I can't believe you all came over here too. I was tryin' to be discreet. What If they heard y'all walkin' over here? Besides, I was planning to tell you everything they said. Now, shh h . . ."

They could hear someone saying "I wonder where she is."

Warren said, "So they have called the police because they said that this isn't her usual behavior. She always lets them know where she is, and what time she'll be back home."

Then, there was a brief silence . . .

"Do you think they quieted down because they know we're all listenin'?"

Francis made a remark about the enormous amount of tension in the next room. She said, "Naw, Willie, I think something else is going on. I wonder what it could be. Things seem to be really tense in there. I hope nothing bad has happened. Our families have had enough. We don't need any more heartbreak."

Dawn then said, "We're bound to find out shortly. You know our parents won't stay silent for long."

Willie then had another idea. "I'm going in there."

Willie's cousin, Junior, doubted that the adults would say a word while Willie was in there.

Willie was just about to step into the next room where the adults were, when unexpectedly, the shattering sound of breaking glass, dispersed into bits and pieces. Willie and the other children, jumped in their astonishment.

With apprehension, Willie opened the door to the den, and when he walked in, he saw that almost everyone had tears in their eyes, and tissues in their hands. Then his mama asked, "Willie, why are you in here?"

"We heard something, mama. It sounded like something broke. What happened? Why is everybody so sad?"

Willie heard a car pulling up in front of the house, so he looked out the window and he saw the police outside with his Uncle James and his Aunt Edna. They were walking towards the house. Uncle James was holding Aunt Edna closely to him, as if he were keeping her from falling. Willie thought Aunt Edna looked like she was going to pass out. Then there was a loud knock at the door. Willie was planning to answer the door, but just as he reached for the door knob, his daddy said, "Uh, Willie, you let me answer the door. I think you should go back in the garage with your cousins."

"Daddy, we all know something's goin' on. Y'all are scarin' us. We're all family and I want to know why everybody's so upset. Is it about Mary Beth? How come she's not here?"

"Willie! Don't disrespect me, and do as I tell you. Go back in the other room."

"Russ! Don't be so hard on him. They're all worried about us. You can tell by the expressions on their faces, that they know something very serious has happened, and they want to know what it is. This is a difficult time for everyone. Willie, a glass broke. That's all," said Maggie. Then she looked at Russ

"Russ, do you want to talk to Willie and the other children now?" asked Maggie.

"No, they'll just have to wait till we're done, and then we'll tell the children what they need to know." Willie then sulked, but he went back to the garage where the others were.

CHAPTER 9

"Don't think that I'm goin' to wait till they tell us anything! Sometimes they just don't understand that we're more grownup than they think we are."

The entire group of kids stayed by the door and listened quietly to the commotion in the next room. When Russ let Edna, James, and the police inside the house, Edna started to fall to the floor. James grabbed her and helped once again to keep her from falling to the ground. Then he picked her up in his arms and carried her to the couch so she could lie down.

Russ asked "What the hell has happened James? What's wrong with Edna? Do we need to call a doctor? You sounded upset on the phone. Now, tell us what's wrong."

Officer Jenkins intervened and without hesitance said, "Russ, now I've known most of you for many years. Will you listen to me, and not just as an officer, but as a friend too? James, do you want me to go ahead and tell them what's happened?"

James looked at Officer Jenkins with tears rolling down his cheeks and told him that he'd tell them himself. Then he could barely say the words, "Our Lori is dead." Then the sheriff helped him to sit comfortably as possible on the sofa beside Edna. She was fully conscious and she was sobbing uncontrollably; understandably so. They had a hole in their hearts that would never heal from the loss of their daughter.

This wasn't the news they hoped to hear. Feeling overwhelmed, the relatives gasped and cried.

Millie asked "What in heaven's name happened to her?"

Officer Jenkins answered, "Millie, we believe it's all part of the killing spree that's been going on these past weeks."

Just then Willie and his cousins stormed into the room and Willie asked "What do you mean these past weeks? Don't you mean these past months? The same killer could be responsible for all the deaths in our home town all these years."

Russ then asked, "What killer, Willie?"

Willie then said, "Well, it could be the *Dirt Man* or even if it ain't him daddy, it could be those giant bats that y'all told us about."

Charles then said, "Well, I don't think it was any giant bats, but I do think that Willie could be right about it being the *Dirt Man*. I think that he might be the one that's been killin' people for years."

Then Russ said, "Willie, I thought I told you to go back in the garage. We don't have time to listen to any nonsense right now."

Then Willie said, "It's not nonsense daddy. You're the one that told us about the bats, and we know that the *Dirt Man* is real. When were y'all goin' to tell us about Lori anyway? We loved her, too. I told that girl to listen to me. Why don't any of the older girls take Charles's and my stories seriously?"

"Well Maggie, I should have listened to you. Willie, I want all of you to listen to me. There's no such thing as giant bats that swoop down from trees at night, steal children, and carry them away. I first made the story up 'cause we wanted y'all to stay on the porch when we visit your great grandma and your great granddaddy. We knew that none of y'all would be tempted to sneak off anywhere if we told you that story. Then some of the relatives and some of our friends told the story to their children; and the next thing you know, almost every parent around here for miles was tellin' that story. Y'all are too old to believe that stuff now.

I do want to hear about this other theory that you kids have though, so what are you talkin' about? *Who in the world is the Dirt Man?* I don't remember hearin' about him before."

"We told you about him before daddy, but you didn't pay any attention either. It's a man that stays dirty all the time 'cause he lives in the woods. Charles and I gave him that name. We believe that he's real daddy." Then Willie glanced over in Charles's direction and asked him what he'd like to add to the conversation.

Charles then said, "Yeah, almost every time somebody disappears or ends up dying, it happens deep in the woods. How about Sammy's car too? That was deep in the woods when he disappeared at night."

"What do you know about Sammy's car being in the woods at night, Willie boy? There weren't any news reports on television that gave that information and now that I think about it, there was an anonymous call one night that led an ambulance and the police to where the car is, but there wasn't a body in the car once we all arrived at the scene. Furthermore, we determined that the car had been moved from within the wooded area to the entrance of the woods. Do you know anything about that, buddy?" Russ was also curious and sternly said "Willie, I told you and Rae Ann that the car was found at the entrance of the woods one morning. You and Rae Ann better tell us whatever y'all know right now! As a matter-of-fact, you, Rae Ann, and Miranda have been acting mighty strange the past few days. Officer Jenkins, I think you ought to question all three of them."

Willie rushed to his mother's side and reached out his arms to hug her. Then he looked up at her with a frightened look on his face. He felt almost as frightened as he did in the woods. Maggie then said, "Now calm down, and tell Officer Jenkins if you know anything. Rae Ann's grandparents gave Rae Ann the same advice. Miranda's parents were angry with Miranda. Her mother said, "We shouldn't have expected to hear anything less than this about you Miranda. Maggie, Miranda hasn't been acting strangely for the past few days. She's been acting like this ever since she was sixteen." Then she said to Miranda, "Go on over there and talk to Officer Jenkins and I'm telling you right now, that you better tell him every detail, because your daddy and me are just about through with you. If you don't start behaving yourself, you're goin' to be on your own as soon as you graduate from high school. We know you're almost eighteen now, but it doesn't give you the right to disrespect us and do whatever you want, whenever you want, and to misbehave when you feel like it."

Edna blurted, "James and me want all of you to just stop fussin'! I mean it! Y'all better stay as close to each other as you can and you better not put Miranda out 'cause you know you all were the same way when you were children. Your time with your child is precious. You hear me?" Then she sobbed once again and said, "I miss our Lori."

"Edna . . . James, we're sorry. We didn't mean to upset y'all. We just didn't want them to hide anything from us."

Willie said, "We wanted to tell, but not yet. We just wanted to learn a few more facts. Who else died?"

Russ said, "Well, we're not sure son. A couple of them are just considered to be missing right now. Mary Beth hasn't been found yet, but her parents told us that the police are checking things out right now. It isn't lookin' too good right now. Now, we're all hoping that Sammy and her did run away and that their parents will hear from them pretty soon. That's why it's important that you and Rae Ann tell us everything; and I mean every little detail about what you and Rae Ann saw."

"We will daddy. You need to talk to Miranda, too. She knows a lot about it, too."

Officer Jenkins said, "Well, buddy, I think you, Rae Ann. And Miranda, better come with me to the police station and we can talk in a little room. How does that sound to you, buddy? There's no need for you to worry right now. We just want to sort things out."

"Does that sound fair to you Rae Ann and to you, Miranda?"

"Yes sir," answered Rae Ann and Miranda.

"All right then. We'll get your statements and we'll have to record everything you three have to tell us."

Willie and the others' eyes widened and he asked, "Are you going to put us in jail?"

"No buddy. The law protects you from that. We just want to do everything properly and according to law."

"Okay. Officer Jenkins, but first, I have to get something out of the closet for you to see."

"All right, buddy."

Willie walked into his bedroom and opened the closet door and pulled his good shoes out. Then he came back to the room with his shoes.

"I have to show my shoes to you and tell you about them, Officer Jenkins. Do you want me to do it now, or down at the police station?"

"Well little buddy, you might as well do it now, since you have them out in open."

Willie looked at his father with apprehension.

"Uh . . . daddy, I'm sorry that I didn't tell you about this earlier."

Then he handed his good Sunday dress shoes over to the officer.

"I wore these the other night when we were in the woods. There's some red stuff on 'em. I was walking, and it got on my shoes. It's all dried up. It looks like blood."

"Have you tampered with them at all?"

"Huh?"

"Never mind. Let me bag it and we'll see what they find out once they're analyzed." Then he walked with one of the other officers to the opposite side of the room and said, "We should be able to find out what blood type this is and maybe whose blood it is."

"I agree. This will get a step closer in the right direction."

"Okay, little buddy, is there anything else you want to tell me before we go?"

"No, I can't think of anything, Officer Jenkins."

"Well, I want to give you three children a few things to think about on the way down to the station; if any of you saw anything strange, you'll need to tell us, or if you were in Sammy's car, and you touched it in any way, your fingerprints will be on the vehicle and we will find your fingerprints. So don't keep anything else to yourselves At this point, it's the worst thing you can do."

"Uh . . . yes, sir. I mean . . . we won't." Then Willie looked up at the sheriff and said, "I touched the car with my hands. I leaned on the car so I could take a closer look at what was inside the car. It looked like blood was on the car seat and Sammy looked like he was sleeping. I don't know how he could sleep, 'cause he looked like he was real cold."

"Okay, now you can wait before you say anything else. Well, are there any more surprises from anybody else, before we go?"

Russ said to Officer Jenkins, "Okay, off the record from one childhood friend to another, Mitch, were you planning to tell us any details about Sammy or Mary Beth, when you came here today? I think we're entitled to know, right now."

"Just stay calm Russ. Your Uncle James and Aunt Edna just wanted to be near y'all and tell you and the others about Lori. I thought it was a good idea that they be near their relatives, and I wanted to come with them in case I could be of assistance to them. I had no idea, whatsoever, that things would escalate to this magnitude. Once, the children started talking, I merely wanted to find out all I could. As you see, we're still trying to leave. If we haven't known and been friends with your family for so long, I would have already hauled every one of you down to the station for questioning an hour ago. Now, is there something else that someone has to tell me right now?"

Francis answered by saying, "Well, yes sir, I do have to tell you something, too."

Everyone in the room was taken by surprise. Francis never did anything unexpected.

"All right Francis, tell us what you know, since you don't think it can wait."

"I was supposed to meet with Lori. We were going to meet some others by the woods, but not in the woods. We were supposed to meet at the entrance on the night of the party and then we were going to leave. We weren't going to walk. We were going to ride in a car with some friends. We didn't see Sammy's car there at all."

Russ belted out "Francis!! I'm surprised at you! What's wrong with you? You know better than that. You're not allowed to go there!"

"I'm sorry daddy. We just figured that there were enough of us hanging out together and didn't think anything bad could happen."

"All right young lady, we'll talk about it down at the station," said Officer Jenkins.

"I have something else to say now."

"Okay Francis, go ahead."

"I'm so sorry Uncle James and Aunt Edna," She was remorseful. Then Aunt Edna reached her arms out to Francis and hugged her too.

Officer Jenkins said to the large group of relatives and friends, "It appears that quite a few of you have secrets to tell."

"Some of us are headed to the police station too; to talk to you about our secrets."

Russ and the others were determined to go with their children and get to the bottom of everything. They also wanted to support their children, and try to take some of their fears away. He just didn't understand why the children didn't confide in him or Maggie in the first place.

"I expected you to feel that way," said Officer Jenkins.

Warren said, "Oh, don't you worry. We're all going to the police station. We're all a package deal. Don't you think for a minute that we're goin' to leave the children alone! They've already been through an awful ordeal and I know they're scared and bothered by all of this. You and the other police need to take it easy on our children."

"Don't let yourself get all upset. The children will be fine. So is . . . everyone's coming? Never mind, I already know the answer to that question. Okay, I guess that's definite. Well, everybody come on then. You might as well."

Millie said, "We'll be with you in a minute. We want to talk to James and Edna for a couple of minutes first. Do you mind?"

"No, Millie, I don't mind. I'll be in the car. I don't know how we're going to fit all of y'all inside the station. I better call in and let them know that they should expect all of you there."

Everyone wanted to console James and Edna and to give them their support and hug them. When Willie's turn came to hug them, he said, "Y'all just have to know that we didn't want to do anything that would upset anybody and remember, we did call an ambulance. Lori wasn't there when we were there. Mary Beth wasn't at the car, either. The last time that we saw Lori, was when we told stories by the campfire in the backyard. Y'all were there too."

"I'm glad you've told us this Willie," said Aunt Edna. Then she hugged him and they cried together. Rae Ann walked over to them and said, "I'm sorry we kept information from everybody. We didn't mean any harm."

Her Uncle James said, "We know that, Rae Ann. Everything is going to be just fine." Then Rae Ann walked over to him and hugged him and Aunt Edna.

When all was said and done, they went outside, stepped into the cars and left for the police station.

Once they entered the police station, one of the deputies asked, "You were serious when you said they were all comin' here, weren't you?"

Officer Jenkins answered, "I'm sure that they wouldn't take *no* for an answer. Now we're stuck with all of 'em that were at the Matthews home. They are good people who have been through a lot, but dealing with them is going to be a huge task. I think I'm going to need a good stiff drink once I'm off duty tonight. Some of you might want to join me too by the time we're done here. Let's get our forms and a recorder now, so we can take statements from these kids and I'm going to find our detectives. Yes siree, it's goin' to be a long day."

"Hey, how long is it going to take, Officer Jenkins? These kids need to take care of their homework for school."

"I don't imagine that any child will go to school for the next few days. It's just too dangerous out there. There'll be an announcement on the news, to keep everyone informed of how things are going to be handled concerning school attendance. The other officers and I will also go to each house, apartment, and every trailer around here to talk to the community and we'll leave notices at every door. As soon as we get organized and make some crucial decisions about protection for all of our children around here, the announcement will be made, so it'll probably be on the evening news. You can hear all about it on the radio, too. The crook's still on the loose, so we don't want to take any chances.

We still don't want any children outside their homes. Unless they're accompanied by at least one parent. Everyone needs to take extreme precaution, no matter what age they are. As far as how long the interrogation will take here today—it shouldn't take too long, if everyone cooperates. I'd say maybe a couple of hours at the most. We've got a couple of detectives that are going to do the majority of the questioning," answered the sheriff.

"They're not suspects are they?" asked Russ.

"No, not by any means, are they considered to be suspects. They're devastated by the news."

"That's agreed on, Russ, and there's no doubt in my mind that they're just victims of circumstances, but we just need the detectives to be convinced of it. I better go in there now, and find out how far they've gotten with the interrogation. Oh, one more thing, before I go in there; will James and Edna stay with someone tonight?"

"Yeah, they'll stay with one of the relatives. I'll be sure to let you know who."

"I appreciate that Russ. I think we're going to have someone watch their house and we'll have one of our officers keep watch wherever they decide to stay tonight, too. Where is Rae Ann stayin' tonight?"

"I think I'll talk to her grandparents about letting her stay with us again. I don't want them mixed up in this anymore than they need to be. They're good folks, and they don't need any stress, so we want to help them all we can."

"We'll have a car or two keep surveillance of your home and Mary Beth's home, too. Why don't you get some coffee 'cause you're not allowed inside with Willie, or with Francis right now. I'm goin' to see how Rae Ann's grandparents are doin'. I don't see any need to question them about it. I want you to listen to me. I want to suggest that you don't keep Rae Ann's grandparents completely out-of-the-loop. They know that there's more to it, than you all have told them. Someone's goin' to have to tell them everything pretty soon. Don't worry either, 'cause they're stronger than they look."

Then Officer Jenkins walked away.

Russ sat down next to Maggie. He was obviously uncomfortable while sitting inside the station, knowing that two of his children were being interrogated.

"Hey, Maggie?"

"What is it, Russ?"

"Do you think Willie's told the story about the bats?"

"Well, it wouldn't surprise me, honey. You should be ashamed of yourself Russ! Will you ever learn?"

"Sure Maggie! I've already learned my lesson. I think most of the folks in Caroline County that you and I grew up with have told that story to their children. Did you see the look on Willie's face when I told him that I made it all up?"

"Yeah, I sure did. They all fell for that bat story. Miranda's almost eighteen years old, and she still believed it. I told her before; some bat stories are myths. Mary Beth believed that story too. They're not even kin to us. It'll probably take more time before they'll truly accept that it's not a true story. They've had the fear of bats for years now. They look up to us and depend on us to tell the truth."

Russ put his arm around Maggie's shoulders and tilted his head near hers and whispered, "Yeah, they're both pretty gullible at times. Those young girls still have some growing up to do."

"Hey look Maggie, there's one of our bat friends outside here, waiting to pick us up and give us a lift home." Then Russ chuckled.

"Oh hush you!" Then she couldn't stop herself from giggling at her husband's little joke. "I guess we can use a little humor right now to keep us from falling apart. I hope we never have to go inside another police station for any reason."

"Here our children come now." Then Russ and Maggie stood up and gave the children a hug.

"I'm a little upset with y'all Willie, since you two didn't tell us that you kids tried to go to the party on your own, but I'm tryin' to put everything into perspective. Your mama and I have to decide how we're going to handle this. I'm sure you know you're in trouble with us now, but don't worry too much 'cause everything is going to be all right just like always."

"Okay daddy. I am real sorry, though."

"We know you are."

"Let's go home now. It's been a long day. We'll go home and get some food and some rest. I have to think about everything that's happened and then we'll talk about the possibility of punishment."

"Are the others goin' home, too, daddy?"

"Well, we might have some company tonight. Millie and Warren might stay another night and your Uncle James and Aunt Edna might spend the night with us or with one of your other relatives. Rae Ann's probably going to spend the night with us, too. So how do you like that?"

"I like it just fine daddy."

My cousins and I hoped that we really would be forgiven for the mischief we got into. We never wanted to disappoint our families for any reason at any time, but when this happened, all we could see was the tremendous disappointment in their eyes and we knew that this situation wasn't going to be forgotten any time soon. We'd certainly understand and accept any punishment that was given to us. Surprisingly though, not another word was said about the whole ordeal to little Willie boy or me for the rest of the day. Come to think of it—they didn't talk to us about anything at all. The trip back from the police station was ridden in silence. They only spoke when we were called to eat our supper and when they told us goodnight. Was this solitude our punishment? We've always been sociable and friendly people. We didn't like this gloomy feeling that came over us when no one would speak to us. We wondered how long it would be before everyone was back to being their cheerful selves again.

Everyone else went back to their homes the next day.

CHAPTER 10

Uncle James and Aunt Edna soon made the funeral arrangements. None of the relatives spoke to each other until the day of the funeral. Everyone wanted Uncle James and Aunt Edna to spend some personal time together to grieve, and take care of things the way they preferred. We heard that an autopsy was performed and we all knew that they didn't want to talk about that. Considering all the pain they were in, the subject of the autopsy was never brought up.

Everyone attended cousin Lori's funeral a few days later. There was so much sadness there. We knew our lives would never be the same again. Lori was Uncle James's and Aunt Edna's only child. Aunt Edna mentioned that she would like to get more involved in all of our lives. Charles heard Aunt Maggie tell Aunt Edna that she knew we'd all get spoiled, knowing how much Uncle James and Aunt Edna love children, but if she wanted to get more involved, it would be fine with her and the others. Maybe it would eventually fill some of the void that she had.

Once the funeral was over, we all went home. Our families called Uncle James and Aunt Edna and took turns bringing some of their favorite meals to their home.

Once matters and emotions subsided, and everyone had time to grieve, my grandma and granddaddy felt that everybody should soon get together again as a family. Aunt Edna wanted our families to stay close and appreciate all we have, and who we have as family, and to always stay close.

Grandma said our relatives made plans to visit. She also said that we could look forward to that instead of worrying about the killer. She thought a murderer would be less likely to hurt any of us when we're all together. She even called him chicken shit. She said that he was worse than the devil, and has tried to make a mess out of our lives; but once the law or one of us gets hold of him, he'd be in one hell of a pickle! She said he'd find out what a mess really is 'cause there ain't goin' to be anything left of him, and that he belongs in prison or in his grave! None of us wanted to let a murderer run our lives, placing this undesirable wedge between us. She said he wasn't man enough to show his face, and that he hides in order to do his dirty work. I never heard my grandma talk like that before, but she was right. I was so happy that we'd all see each other soon. So even though the visit was delayed, we knew we'd all see each other again and be together as one; bonded and feeling as strong as ever; not letting anyone come between any of us. This murderer must have thought he was clever, but in our minds, he used no intelligence at all. He could never break our family apart.

Some people learn in life that sometimes lessons can be learned through tragedies. This tragedy involving our cousin Lori brought our relatives even closer together. Our mama even came home once she learned what happened. She stayed in Virginia, for about a month. It wasn't long enough, but even so, she was there with Ray, and Sue and me. Everything felt complete once again. Even when she left (as she always did), she stayed in constant contact with us; at least once a week. She didn't want us to ever feel like she didn't love us. She told us that she hadn't found us a new father yet, or a better job, but when she did, she'd be back again to stay. At that time, we weren't sure if that was the whole truth or not, but one thing's for sure, she really did love us; the only way she knew how and we loved her, too.

So the awaited day came—about three weeks later, our relatives pulled up in the Corvair, the Pontiac, the Firebird, the pickup truck, and the Mustang, in front of our house. I used to love to watch all the cars pull up and count the number of people that came to see us.

It was a beautiful, sunny day and it was as if nothing terrible had even happened. Everyone exchanged their hugs and hellos and then went inside.

First, everyone sat in our family room and talked about their plans for the day. Then, the fun began. Granddaddy unfolded the card table, got a deck of cards out. Playing a game of cards was what the men enjoyed most, when they all got together. Little Willie always sat under the table and picked up the coins as they fell to the floor. He could always count on coins fallin' because the livelier things got, the more relaxed, and the more the men drank during the card game, assured Charles and Willie that the better the chances were that money would fall in abundance to the floor. Cousin Charles was older and a bigger boy than Willie, but it didn't stop him from sometimes tryin' to fit under the table. Once he realized that he was just too big, he let Willie pick up the loose change. They counted the money and split it between them. Those boys would walk around and tell everybody that they were rich.

While most of the men played cards, some of our other folks played horseshoes outdoors, and some of the women cooked in the kitchen. Once the food was ready, we'd all sit around the table together.

After lunch, granddaddy always picked up his guitar. Uncle James even brought his guitar to the house as he always did, and joined in as they played and sang "Your Cheatin' Heart." Everybody joined in with the music. One day I told granddaddy that he and Uncle James sound like country music stars. "I don't know about all that, but if Rae Ann thinks we do, then maybe we should put on a show for everybody."

I replied, "Sure . . . Y'all are the best in the world." Then they taught my cousins and me how to play some chords. I'll never forget how close we all felt.

———————————

Willie said, "Hey, Rae Ann? We need to go outside and have a talk."

Uncle Russ was a little concerned about us goin' outdoors, but since the police were supposed to watch the house for us, he decided that it might be all right as long as we stayed in the yard.

Willie and the rest of us gathered the lawn chairs together and sat in a circle beside the house, and then Willie picked up a couple of things from the ground and took some pieces of paper out of a bag that he had brought with him.

"Willie, what are you holding in your hand?" I asked. We were very curious.

"My nerves are all torn up, Rae Ann. Y'all know when the grownups want something to calm their nerves, they drink or they smoke. I just think that I need to calm my nerves a little bit. I brought enough for all of us. I crumbled up some leaves and I cut some paper into squares. I'm goin' to roll 'em up and we can pretend that we're smokin' cigarettes. Now who wants to join me in smokin' a cig or maybe you want a little swig?"

"Well, I don't know Willie. We'll have to see you do it first."

Then I looked and asked "Willie? You're not goin' to light that thing up are you?"

"Naw, Rae Ann. I told you that we're all just goin' to pretend that we're smokin'."

Cousin Charles then said, "Hmm . . . that's good 'cause I was just going to tell you that you better be careful with that boy 'cause you don't want to burn up anything. Mama and daddy just might want to whip your tail if you really lit that up."

"Don't worry Charles. I'm just pretending so I can feel like I'm relaxing."

"Well, what can we have a swig of?"

"You'll see."

"Okay then. It amazes me when I think about how many crazy ideas that you come up with," said Charles.

"This ain't a new idea. I learned it from daddy and his friends. Some of the women do it sometimes too; except none of them are pretending to do it."

Then the rest of us decided to join in with Willie. He rolled the bits of leaves into the paper squares and since the paper wouldn't stick together, he decided to hold it together with glue. Then we each took one.

Then Willie pulled out the cans. Dawn asked, "Great Day! What have you got now Willie? What are you doin' with beer cans? Is anything in 'em?"

"No, you silly girl. They're all empty. I took them out of the bin in the basement."

"Ooooh Willie, you are gonna get in trouble with mama and daddy. You know they get money for that stuff."

"I only took enough cans for all of us. Then I'm goin' to take them back home and put 'em back inside the bin."

"I guess that will be all right then."

So then Willie picked up a jug with something in it.

Then I said, "Well cousin, what's in the jug? Just what did your sneaky self-find to put in the cans?"

We all waited, anxiously, for him to tell us what it was.

"It's apple juice. What in the world did you think it was?"

We all laughed.

Then, Willie poured the juice into the beer cans. Once that was done, he decided to talk about some things.

As usual, he talked about the *Dirt Man*. My cousin Willie's whole purpose for the discussion with us was for us to make a pact. I remember that he wanted each of us to write down any new information that we came across, concerning the murders, and anything unusual. We all made a pact that day, to stick together to find the murderer.

Willie already knew the total number of victims that disappeared, and the total number that the police knew was murdered, He never wanted to exclude any names, for as long as it would take to catch the killer. He had all sorts of notes.

I asked Willie if he thought we'd catch the *Dirt Man* soon and he told me that he thought we would, but if we didn't, he'd never give up trying.

That wasn't a difficult promise for any of us to make or to keep. We wanted nothing more than to catch him. We all shook hands and swore to keep our pact a secret; at least for a while.

Well, we ended our meeting and stayed outdoors. We laughed and talked until we heard Uncle Russ yell, "What are y'all doin' out here? We can't leave y'all alone for a dern minute anymore."

Aunt Maggie and the rest of them hurried outdoors. Aunt Maggie said, "Mercy! Have y'all lost your minds?"

Willie said, "Now wait a minute! Don't get the wrong idea. We ain't doin' anything wrong."

Russ belted out, "What do you mean y'all ain't doin' anything wrong? What's the matter with you boy? We decided to let y'all come outside and we trusted y'all. Couldn't you behave yourself—especially after the hell we've all been through? Haven't you learned anything? I have just about had it with you. Your mama and me are at our wits' ends. What have you got to say for your selves?"

"Daddy, what I'm tryin' to tell you, is that it ain't what you think. We're just tryin' to relax. My nerves are bad, so I just wanted to help my cousins and me to try to relax and enjoy ourselves, just like y'all do."

"With cigarettes?"

"Naw daddy, these ain't cigarettes. I crumbled up leaves and rolled them up in some paper. Look daddy." Then he handed one of them to his father. Willie looked straight into his eyes and then he looked straight into his mama's eyes with his uplifted eyebrows, and his big brown eyes, and said, "When y'all want to relax, y'all smoke cigarettes and sometimes y'all drink. I knew y'all be upset with us if we did that, so I made some pretend cigarettes and took some empty beer cans out of the bin in the basement. There's no beer in them. Y'all already rinsed them out and I rinsed them out too. I bought some apple juice with some money I had and poured it into the jug. We just wanted to act like y'all grownups. We didn't mean any harm. I didn't think anything was wrong with it since y'all do it. Besides, our stuff ain't even real."

Suddenly, there was a screeching sound coming from out on the street. A car sped down the road. Willie and his cousins jumped at the sound of it.

Russ looked at the frightened looks on their faces. He decided to talk to the kids instead of punishing them. He was almost at a total loss of words. After carefully thinking about what his answer would be, he finally said, "Your mama and your aunts have been wanting the other guys and me to quit smoking and drinking or to at least slow down."

Then he barely had enough courage to look at Maggie. Instead, he just brushed his hand over his head and stroked his fingers through his hair a couple of times because he felt a little fidgety and awkward, knowing that this wasn't the image that he wanted his children, or any of the other children to have of him. He didn't want any of their adult friends or relatives to have this sort of reputation either.

Maggie said, "Yeah that's right. Well Russ, let us chalk up another one for you and the guys. You've all earned the reputations through the years of being a little wild and now the children want to act just like y'all. Do you believe that you men will finally start listening to us more about these things?"

"I believe we will," replied Russ.

Edna asked, "Well, how about the rest of y'all?"

Blake, James, Warren, and the rest of the men promised that they would start listening to their wives more often, especially since their fun tended to have a way to backfire on them more times than they could count.

"We're all here for you kids. If any of you are worried, nervous, or upset about anything, y'all can talk to us. You all know that already."

Then I said, "Well, y'all know that I like to sing songs and write poems. Music and poetry always make me feel better."

"Yeah, and some of us like to go fishing, but we can't do that at the pond 'cause what if that *Dirt Man*'s there?"

"All right Willie, that's enough. We don't want to hear anything about that today."

"But daddy, you said we can talk to y'all if we need to."

"Willie! I meant what I said. Okay? I just don't want things to get stirred up any more than they already are. Let's just stay off of that subject right now."

"Okay, daddy, but can we talk about him soon?"

Russ then answered, "Yeah, I reckon so, Willie."

"Thanks. Daddy, you're not upset with me are you? We don't have to go in the house now do we?" asked Willie.

"No, I just want this to be a pleasant day. You don't have to go in the house since I know what's goin' on out here. You never cease to amaze me, son." Russ then turned his head from side to side in dismay. "Now, I'm going to be honest with each of you. We're probably not going to stop smokin' or drinkin' completely, but we do plan to slow down and we won't do it around any children anymore. You kids have to think about other ways to occupy your selves too. Y'all also need to think about something else. It's the law that you have to be of age to drink alcohol and to smoke cigarettes, so don't y'all ever play like that again. Other people might not know that you're just pretending. It's too misleading. Do you understand me?"

"Yeah daddy; I know that we all understand that."

"That's quite a boy and quite a handful that you've got there Russ. He's definitely a Matthew's boy," remarked James. "He's almost a splittin' image of you."

Everyone agreed with James.

"James is right. Come to think of it, you were a lot like that when you were his age Russ," said Millie. "You remember don't you?"

"Are you tryin' to be funny again sis or are you serious?"

"A little of both, Russ. It ain't anything to be concerned about. You turned out to be a good man, and so will young Willie."

"I'm not concerned about it, and I'm pretty proud of that boy. I told you that before," said Russ.

Maggie noticed the time and said, "Okay, it's not going to be dark for another hour or so, so how about we all play a game of croquette for a change?"

Francis exclaimed "Great mama!" Then they all played croquette and played ball, too. When they were done, they went back inside the house, ate dinner, and sang some more songs together. They decided to spend the entire evening there.

The next morning, after breakfast—they said their goodbyes to one another. They were just about to step outside, when suddenly they heard a loud noise. It sounded like something had been smashed. There was broken glass on the street. Once outside, they discovered that someone had thrown something through one of the car windows.

"This kind of stuff never happens around here, but it just happened to one of your car windows Blake. Don't worry, we'll find the nut who did that 'cause we all know that we're not goin' to let something like that go."

"You're right about that. I have no intentions of lettin' it go, but at least I know that I can fix it. I am a mechanic, so I can fix the window pretty cheap," said Blake. "I'm not even going to fool with the insurance on it. Don't worry one little bit, though, 'cause I'll make him pay for the damage one way or another, Russ. I can handle it," said Blake.

"I know you can, Blake, but we'll take care of it together. Right now, we need to report it to the police." said Russ.

"Where are they? I thought the police were goin' to keep an eye on things!"

Blake noticed something peculiar, but familiar, on the ground and he bent down and picked it up.

"Hey, this is a bullet casing. This wasn't any accident, but I don't have any enemies as far as I know. Damn it! This ain't no joke! Somebody's out to hurt someone!" Then the men told the women and children to go back inside and that's exactly what they did.

Then Blake said, "For the life of me—I can't think of a soul who would do something like this. Now I'm starting to wonder if anybody is truly safe anywhere. This is starting to get awfully personal."

The police came, and feeling very frustrated, Russ said, "I thought y'all were supposed to keep our families under surveillance. Why didn't you see what happened? You should have caught the son-of-a-bitch that did this to Blake's car."

"I'm sorry sir, but this is a different jurisdiction. We didn't have all the paperwork done from Caroline or Port Royal, but let me assure you that we're going to be on top of things to keep everyone safe from harm." Then they took pictures, took the bullet casing, asked a few questions, wrote a report, and told them that they'd be in contact.

"Well, we've done all that we can do about this today," said James. "We can't let this bother us right now 'cause I think that's what the crook wants. He wants things to just fester inside us until we breakdown. We can't let him have what he wants. It just gives him too much satisfaction to suit me."

"Yeah, you're right. We can't let him have his way," said Russ. "All right, let's just figure out what we're going to do a little bit later. For now, we'll let the police handle it."

"Blake, do y'all want to spend another night here tonight?" asked Rae Ann's grandfather. "We'll be glad to have you here."

Then Elsie and Edna, Maggie, Millie, along with the rest of them popped their heads out the door from inside the house. One of them decided to answer for all of them. "We'd love to."

She wasn't sure if it was a good idea for any of them to go home that day.

"No, we'll just go home," said Blake. "Don't y'all worry."

"Well, we can't help worrying Blake, so just stay here for one more night. We'll feel a whole lot better if y'all do."

"I think it would be better if you stay here until you hear from the police again."

"I think you better listen to him. You know he's older and has more experience than the rest of us."

Maggie said, "Well, I also think you better listen to him and I'm not going to take no for an answer, either. It would be better for everybody to be together. You already know that. We'll all wait to hear what the police have found out for us and if they say it's all right to go home tomorrow, we can all go."

"Well, I don't mind expressing my opinion, so let me tell y'all that by the time y'all finish talkin' this out, it'll be dark anyway and we've still got just one more day left in the weekend, so please just hurry up and make up your mind," said Edna.

Blake winked and said, "Well, come on—what are we waitin' for? Bring the beer out and let's play some cards!"

"Well, then it's settled; we'll all unpack our bags and have a good time."

"You said it!" exclaimed granddaddy. "Yee haw! We're glad you're all here."

"None of us wanted you to have any trouble," remarked Russ.

"It ain't a problem a 'tall," answered Rae Ann's granddaddy as he spoke in his deep-rooted country manner.

"Now the police are aware of everything, so I don't think that nut will pull anything tonight 'cause somebody would catch him. Now, come on downstairs, and let's play cards."

So they all spent one more night at our house. We all felt so close and although, there was more trouble, the bond that our relatives shared, made it another one of the happiest days we ever spent together.

CHAPTER 11

Rae Ann then thought back to the book that Willie wrote in every time everyone got together. It was a lot like a diary, but this book had very specific information in it. Each of the cousins kept information, but Willie's book had very detailed information in it.

Cousin Willie kept information about every situation he knew about and everything he thought was related to the *Dirt Man*. He wrote information in it almost daily. Even if the day was just a typical day in Caroline, he'd write that there were no signs of the *Dirt Man* that particular day.

He wrote the date and the times of each occurrence. He had the counties, the towns, the specific places with the names of the roads. He wrote every detail that he possibly could. He hoped to personally make sure this killer paid for everything he did to each victim. Willie's book was put to good use for many years. It kept Willie and others fully informed.

Uncle Russ always told Willie what he knew about any current crimes, especially murders; although he sometimes questioned why Willie wanted that information. Willie kept the reason to himself, rather than tell Uncle Russ, knowing that his daddy didn't want him consumed with this. It was already past that point. Willie was never going to give up. It still wasn't known at that time, if Sammy was murdered, and was beyond a doubt, the boy who was inside the El Camino. Forensic testing was still being done. There was very little evidence found concerning Mary Beth; what was found, was contaminated. Everyone suspected that the bear made a meal out of her.

A few more years passed, and Willie, who was now a teenager, still kept count of every murder and abduction that happened in their town and in all the surrounding areas. There were no reports of felonious types of crimes in their community for almost six years; not on television or from any other resource that was available to Willie and his family and friends. Everyone was relieved that these crimes had subsided; at least for the time being, and because of this, some of the town's folk felt that it was probably safe to camp and swim and fish in the wooded areas again; areas which included some of their favorite campgrounds, where they all loved to spend a lot of their time in previous years.

One weekend, Willie's two best friends who were Steve Mills and Tommy Grayson, told Willie that their families were going camping for the weekend. When they told him where, they didn't get the kind of reaction that they expected from Willie. He was bothered by the news because as far as he was concerned, they still needed to stay away from there at least long enough to search for more clues. He was sure that there was still an encumbrance of clues buried within the bushes or embarked on tree limbs or even hidden in the tall grass. He still remembered stepping in the thick, slippery, red-tinted mud from his first experience with the *Dirt Man*. The red color was actually traces of blood that had seeped into the mud. It turned out to be positive findings of Sammy's DNA. This was going to be used to convict the killer. With this kind of evidence, how could the police just quit their search? Why wasn't anyone arrested? Willie heard someone talk about something getting contaminated. He wondered if they were referring to the blood. The *Dirt Man* had once again eluded the police. Willie wanted them to find all the clues that could lead the police to the capture of the killer. But time went on and everything about it was pretty much swept under the rug. No one spoke much about it at all anymore. It all remained a mystery.

Willie looked at the two of his buddies and implored that they talk to their parents about camping somewhere else. There's an abundance of beautiful wooded areas and campgrounds in Virginia. The picturesque nature is breathtaking. Willie persuaded them to ask about camping in the Shenandoah Valley area, mentioning that the Blue Ridge Mountains or Luray Caverns would be incredible places to camp.

Willie said, "Don't y'all want to see the stalagmites and the stalactites at Luray Caverns? We haven't been there since our school trip in elementary school. Your parents would enjoy it there. Maybe you could tell them that it's time for them to explore their horizons."

Steve spoke up and said, "Sure Willie. I'll never forget goin' there. We didn't want to leave. It was a lot of fun, but if I tell them to explore their horizons, they'll know that you said that."

Being the close friends that they were, they both assured Willie that they would indeed, talk to the parents about changing their plans. They liked nothing more than to go back to Luray Caverns, but they knew in their hearts that it didn't matter at all where they camped as long as they could all pal around together and have a great time.

Willie said, "Well, your parents didn't ask me to go, so maybe they can go and you boys can spend the weekend at my house."

"Of course you're invited Willie. Since when has anybody ever had to ask you? You've always gone with us camping. It wouldn't be the same without you. When did you let this kind of stuff bother you so much?"

"Well, since my encounter with the *Dirt Man* on the night of the Tallhouse's party. Luckily, Rae Ann and I got out of those woods in the nick of time. Mary Beth wasn't so lucky. You know that we haven't seen her since that night."

"Willie, don't you let that discourage you! She'll be found someday. Now, let's talk about our camping trip."

So, a couple more days went by, and then Willie and his friends met up with one another between classes and wouldn't you know it, neither one of them could persuade their parents to camp anywhere else, and they decided to personally ask Willie to come along, too. Steve's and Tommy's parents just didn't think there was any reason to be concerned. They told Willie that everyone would remain pretty close together and that they'd be involved in activities together and wherever they went and no matter what they did, they'd be in pairs or in groups. Willie didn't agree with their way of thinking at all, but he wasn't about to decline on his invitation to go there with his friends. He was very protective of everyone that he cared about, so he told them that they could count him in. He was going to try hard to have some real fun too.

"Yeah, give it a rest Willie. You do know that the campground over there isn't the only campground where murders occurred. If it is the *Dirt Man* that's doin' all these things, he's moving around from place to place 'cause he's trying to make it hard for them to know exactly where he can be found. Sparta, Bowling Green, Milford, and a few other towns have had these problems too and we've gone to all of 'em. We know how you feel and we're inclined to agree with you, but we gave it our best shot. You know how parents are sometimes," said

Tommy. "Don't worry. They said that everything would be fine. We're goin' to have a real cool time. I'm tired of feeling scared all the time. Aren't you?"

"Yeah, I am," said Willie. "Okay, let's make our plans."

Little did they know that more news of mysterious disappearances on those old dirt roads had surfaced around the town, during a time that they were trying to set aside their fears that had engrossed them more than anyone could even imagine in their young, innocent lives. The naive boys didn't know that this visit to the countryside off Route 17, just north of Port Royal, might be another one of the gloomy, traumatic, and vivid horrors that would be embedded in their thoughts, and in their memories. Willie, his cousin Rae Ann, and no one else in Caroline would ever forget.

Willie went home from school and told his daddy, Russ and his mama Maggie about his invitation. They thought it was a good idea to let Willie go camping. They thought it would help him forget some of those dark days of his past experiences.

Russ said, "Willie, You go ahead and go with them. As a matter-of-fact, we'll probably head on over there this weekend too and meet up with all y'all. It'll be like the good ol' days. You and I will go fishin' and everything. If I catch more fish than you, you'll have to clean 'em. How does that sound son?"

"Fishing sounds like a good plan to me daddy, but you know that I'm goin' to catch the most fish. I'm the king when it comes to catchin' fish," answered Willie.

"Only because I taught you, so that just makes you the prince of fish catchin'. You know I'm the real king of fishin'.'"

Willie thought if anything bad did happen, he'd like nothing better than to be with his friends and family. They could all be there for moral support.

The news of the families' plans to camp out spread like a grapevine. Maggie decided to call Russ's sister Millie and invite her and Warren, and by the end of the day, every relative of theirs had planned to go camping with them, too. Willie decided he wouldn't worry needlessly again. Maybe it was going to be just the way that Steve's and Tommy's folks said.

Well, Friday finally got here and Steve's parents were in one car with the camping gear in the trunk, and the coolers with the food and drinks and miscellaneous apparatus in the backseat. Willie, Steve, and Tommy rode with Tommy's parents and followed in the car behind them. Russ and the others were going there a little later that afternoon.

Soon we all were there. Some pitched tents and some stayed in trailers that remained on the campgrounds all year long, and two of the families drove their mobile homes to the campgrounds. The boys and girls brought their bicycles, radios, dirt bikes, balls, gloves, and cameras with them. Willie brought his little book with him—*just in case.*

It was about 9 pm Friday evening, in April, and we all sat around the campfire and sang some country songs and danced and told some humorous stories. Humorous stories were told since younger children were there. It was a new rule that scary stories could not be told to any of the younger children at any time. Besides, funny stories might keep everyone in a happy frame of mind. They didn't want any of them to be fearful for any reason. Willie was a little tempted to make comments about the shadows that seemingly moved about them as they sat around the fire with its flickering flames, but he was reminded of the "no scary story" rule and told a joke instead. Everyone was pleased to see that Willie was starting to act the way he used to; funny and bursting with a lot of bright, colorful personality. It was indeed, a great night for everybody. Everyone finally turned in for the night around midnight. They hoped to wake up early the next morning for all the activities that they planned to do.

Very early the next morning, everything still appeared to be in the norm for everybody. We ate breakfast and we were all divided up into pairs and told that under no circumstances, whatsoever, was anyone allowed to leave the one they were paired up with. Willie then had a question or two. Willie asked, "What if an emergency happens? What do we do then? What if it's the *Dirt Man*? We'll need some sort of weapon to tear his butt up won't we?" All the kids agreed with Willie (that's no surprise).

Willie's mama, Maggie, then said, "Willie, there's no reason for alarm." Then Russ added, and will you forget about that dern so-called *Dirt Man*, boy? Don't scare the little ones."

"That's right. We're just talking about the usual things that you do for safety. We don't want anyone going too far away, so we'll have to set some perimeters."

One of the younger children asked, "Set some what?"

Maggie repeated herself and said, "Perimeters. For example, Tara, and the rest of you that are eleven years old and younger won't be allowed to go on the dirt bike paths and you'll have to be where an adult can see you and as for you teenagers, we're counting on each of you to use good judgment and serious precaution. If someone has an accident, you'll have to call one of us for help. Thank goodness we have enough walkie-talkies for everybody."

Russ also wanted the teenagers to know that he agreed with Maggie, and he didn't feel that there was a need for any kind of weapons. "Remember to just keep your mind on what you're doing and drive your dirt bikes safely. Stay in designated areas only! The signs are marked for riding dirt bikes, and please don't hesitate to call for help if anything does happen. If you all stay together and stay focused, nothing should go wrong. Even if a criminal was on the loose, that crook would be a fool to even think about messing around with any one of us. He better not think about comin' around here, corrupting things. Listen. We don't want y'all to stay out there late. Also, we want y'all to call us at least once an hour I think we'll all feel better then. There's one other thing that I'd like to add—no one is to walk alone anywhere in the woods at any time. You can hang out together in groups or with the one you were paired up with or with someone else; just not alone."

Everyone took Russ's words quite seriously.

"Yeah, that nut would be *one sorry soul* if he thought even for a second that he'd get away with harming any one of them. He'd run for the hills or wish he were dead," Russ whispered to Maggie and then Maggie nodded her head in agreement with him.

Steve and Tommy were paired up together and Willie and me, Rae Ann, were paired up together. Luckily, there was an even number of kids, so everyone ended up with one other person. We planned to go dirt biking riding later that day. That morning, we just wanted to swim, so walked to the pond.

After looking around at the familiar surroundings, Willie said, "Okay, let's all hang close together. This is starting to feel just a little bit eerie."

"Yeah, kinda déjà-vu, huh Willie?" remarked Rae Ann. It reminds me a little bit like that time we sneaked to the party, walking on the old dirt paths.

"Yeah, things couldn't feel much creepier than this Rae Ann," said Willie.

Tommy said, "Hey you two, quit it now. I remember you tellin' us about that, but let's make this a good day by tryin' to have a good time. You know that nothing like what happened that night has happened for a long time now."

"You're right Tommy," said Rae Ann, "but you know what? I'd feel better if I could sing a song right now." Then she sang the words:

> *It's cryin 'time no more.*
>
> *We'll carry on with our lives,*
>
> *Just the way we did before.*
>
> *You can just leave us alone,*
>
> *And let it be known,*
>
> *That it's cryin' time no more.*

Then we all sang that song until the pond came into view.

Tommy said, "Now, come on, I'll race ya the rest of the way."

"You're on, Tommy!" exclaimed Willie. Then we all ran and Steve ran faster than any of us. He was the first to jump in and then Willie, Tommy, and me, Rae Ann. I wasn't too far behind. Rae Ann thought about how they plunged into the chilly pond, making a big splash and the droplets of water sprayed up into the air like an enormous fountain and poured down on the four of them as they stroked their way back up to the surface and swam. They felt some of the zest that they had when they were even younger children. The water was refreshing and it brought smiles to each of their faces. They had no worries that day because they just lived for the moment rather than dwell on the past. After a couple of hours, they decided to get out of the water and sit on the grass along the side of the pond.

"That was fun. It's always fun to take a dip over here after a long day at school. It's a dern shame that we can't do that anymore," said Rae Ann.

Then Tommy said, "I'm glad we came and maybe we will be able to do that again. If nothing bad happens here, our parents might let us come back again. Things are great right now. Maybe everything will stay that way."

Like always, with his suspicious nature, Willie still had concerns about the *Dirt Man*. As usual, the *Dirt Man* was still on his mind since he hadn't been caught yet. He really didn't want to let the others know, but he decided to confide in Rae Ann about it. He nudged her with his elbow and whispered to her, saying, "Hey cousin, do you think the *Dirt Man's* here? Are you thinking about that night?" She nodded her head up and down. Both Willie and Rae Ann thought for a moment about their friend Mary Beth and how much they've missed her. Even though she agitated them at times, they still considered her to be their friend. They wondered if she'd ever be found. Up to this point, nothing that frightening has happened to Miranda since that night, but at times, she still felt like someone was watching her every movement.

They were eating snacks when they heard some noise. Steve asked, "Did any of you hear anything back there in the trees?"

All of them had, but they didn't want to panic.

Rae Ann said, "It's probably just some birds or some animal running around back there. I'm just feelin' too good from our day together. Look—I'm not shaking at all from the noise in the woods." She lifted her arms upward for them to see for themselves. "I could make up another song if y'all want me to; if y'all are feelin' a little bit nervous."

Willie said, "Naw, there's no need to sing right now 'cause we're not nervous. I think the noise we hear could be a bird or a fox, scuffling around, but I think we ought to consider heading back to camp. If any of you want to get some rest before we go out on the bikes, you should do it right after lunch. It's almost time to eat right now and you know that we don't want to miss out on any of that good food."

"Yeah, we're going do some good eatin' this weekend with all the women cooking. There will be plenty to eat all weekend long and we'll have enough to bring back home with us, too," said Steve.

"That's for sure," said Tommy. Then they got up and decided to race back to the campsite. Everybody ate all they possibly could and then they slept. Shortly after their naps, they joined in on family activities that included playing games of horseshoes, and catch, and a couple of races that were done on foot with four teams competing against one another.

CHAPTER 12

There were still a few hours of daylight left, so the teens got on their dirt bikes. They could go, but they were reminded to ride in pairs, and to hold on to their walkie-talkies, and flashlights. Their parents knew that if they had their flashlights with them they could see and if they had their walkie-talkies, they could communicate. After they got their gear together, their helmets and their gloves on, and their knee pads on, they took off, down the long stretch of winding, hilly dirt paths. The paths were perfect to ride on. They could hardly wait to feel the breeze go through their hair and the adrenalin rush.

They started out riding together as a group, one behind the other. "These paths aren't that bad. You know that we can handle the ride with no trouble," said Steve, as he shook his head with confidence. They enjoyed every minute until they separated, because that's when things started turning a little strange. The path branched out into two separate paths. Two pairs of teens rode their bikes on one of the paths and four other pairs went on the other path.

"Let's just ride a little longer. It's getting' dark out here," said Steve. He also heard some of the same eerie sounds that he heard when he was with Willie, Tommy, and Rae Ann earlier that day at the pond.

Tommy and Steve drove their dirt bikes directly behind Rae Ann and Willie when they first started out, but then Tommy and Steve, trying to be daredevils, passed right by them. They exclaimed as they went passed, "We'll meet you two turtles back at the campsite! Woooo! Clean out of sight baby! Hear my loud *roarrrrrrr*!"

Rae Ann said, "Willie, did you hear what they called us? Now they're in for it. Just wait till we catch up with them." Then she laughed. They sped up a little more, but not fast enough to catch up with them, like they hoped.

Minutes later, they heard a crash and the sound of their friends' dirt bikes faded into the sound of only one dirt bike. Then they heard somebody yelling. It sounded like Tommy's voice. When they saw Tommy, he was alone. Steve's dirt bike was on the ground.

Willie said, "Are you two playin' around? Come on! You know this kind of stuff upsets us. Now, where's Steve?"

"I'm not tryin' to play any kind of game with y'all. I wouldn't do that. I'm tellin' you that he's not here. After we rode by you and Rae Ann, Steve slammed into a big rock. It was covered up with leaves and small twigs. There's no way that he could have seen the rock. Steve went right into it. He lost control of his bike and it went up in the air with him on it, and he landed in one spot and the bike landed right here where we're standing. It looks as if he might have landed just over there by that tree. See? You can see some of the tire tracks on the path from his bike and there's his wallet on the ground. It's about four or five feet away from us."

Rae Ann asked, "Why in the world are we still standing here then? We need to walk over there and look for him."

"I just looked before y'all got here. He's not there," said Tommy.

"We'll have to see if there are any footprints," Willie said. His desperation to find some clues was apparent. They decided to look together, but they only found tire tracks.

"Why can't we find any footprints? I just don't understand. Somebody had to be here, already waiting for y'all or someone else to come along. That's the only way there was enough time to grab Steve. We've got to find somethin'. Let's look a little bit longer."

Not a clue was found.

Willie panicked and said, "See, I told you Tommy. Nobody should be here, at these campgrounds until they catch the *Dirt Man*. The kidnappings are happening all over again."

"What are we going to do?"

"What do you mean—what are we going to do, Tommy? We're going to call my daddy and Steve's folks. You know everybody's going to come and find out what's goin' on."

Rae Ann said, "We have to get on the walkie-talkies and call everybody right now. They need to come and take a look and they'll call the police."

Tommy was overcome by sadness and guilt.

"Tommy, snap out of it. You didn't do anything wrong except the usual mischief that you, me and Steve get into. Don't worry 'cause you two stayed on the trails. I just knew something like this was going to happen again. Didn't I? Why would anyone even question my opinions about these things? I've been keeping track of this killer for many years now. It might even be more than one killer. I've got all the information in my book. You see? It's right here. I have specific, detailed information. You all know that. You all were supposed to keep notes about it too. So where are your notes?"

"Okay, Willie. I know . . . I know and I'm sorry. Listen—I do have notes about the *Dirt Man;* but, I don't write my info down every time something happens. I should, though. I feel real bad about not camping somewhere else, but you know I tried to talk my parents out of campin' here, Willie. They didn't listen."

"I know Tommy. You guys tried to do what I asked—which was the right thing to do. There's nothing more that you or Steve could do to persuade your parents to forget about coming here, and I know you're just as upset about it as I am. We'll just have to hope that he'll outwit the *Dirt Man* and find a way to get away from him. Well, now it's time to tell everybody what's happened."

So Rae Ann made the call and within a few short minutes, everyone left the site and as quickly as they could and met up with the teens.

"What happened?" asked Steve's parents. Tommy told them, and Steve's mother burst into tears.

"Mr. Mills? Is she going to be all right?" asked Tommy as he sobbed. "I don't know what happened to him. He just hit that rock and flew into the air, landed, and then he was gone. He couldn't have seen that rock. It was covered up."

Mr. Mills said, "It sounds like you kids did everything you were told, so it's not your fault. I wish you stayed with the group, but at least you stayed in pairs. The only thing we can do now is call the police and look for him." Then he put his hand on Tommy's shoulder to comfort him.

The police were called immediately. The FBI and the CSI also arrived. Everyone was questioned. A search was performed and Steve's wallet was taken for evidence. They took samples of the soil and planned to get fingerprints from Steve's wallet, although they'd probably only find Steve's fingerprints. They agreed with Willie; that the one who abducted Steve most likely did plan everything out and was probably already waiting for the dirt bike accident to occur. They checked thoroughly for footprints, but they saw no footprints in the area. It got very late in the evening. Everyone walked closely together, but somehow, during that same evening, there was another disappearance. They all went back to their campsite; once the police told them that they would continue the search the next day, and when everyone got ready to turn in for the night, it was noticed that Tommy, who was just going to Willie's tent to say goodnight, disappeared into the night also. Everyone's tents, trailers, and mobile homes were within a few feet of each other, so no one understood how someone could manage to take Tommy away. It wasn't noticed until very early, the next morning. The Grayson family thought their son was with Willie, and Willie thought Tommy was with his parents.

The police weren't far away and they were again called back to the campsite. They didn't know how they could miss seeing anyone enter the area. A search was performed by the police and the FBI only that day. At first, the relatives even started to suspect each other since it appeared that no one else was at their campsite—as far as they knew that is. They soon dropped their suspicion of one another because they knew each other so well and knew how much they loved and cared about each other. They realized that they could even be possible suspects of the FBI since there weren't any leads at the time. They soon learned that other campers nearby, who were in the area, were also interrogated and their names were added to the law officials' lists also.

At this point, Willie didn't even trust the police. For a few moments, he wondered if that was why the police never caught anyone; because, one or more of them could be involved in the disappearances and murders. He wrote down his new curiosities about it, but soon let go of his suspicions about the police.

So after all the questions, the search which involved many hours of looking in every place they could, the police and the FBI told everyone that they would be in contact with them but for now they needed to go home. The wooded areas in Port Royal and all surrounding areas were once again forbidden to all residents.

CHAPTER 13

A couple of weeks later, another friend of Willie's whose name was Rex Wells, went to Willie's home to visit and to find out if there was any more information about their friends' disappearance.

Willie said, "You know that our campgrounds are the best campgrounds around here. There's a history that involves General Robert E. Lee, General Ulysses S. Grant, and the Civil War, from back in 1864 and 1865; that we learned about in school. It's called the North Anna Campaign. General Lee and General Grant first met in battle near the campgrounds. The trails there lead to five sites in Caroline County, where we have the town of Bowling Green, Bethel Church, Carmel Church, Guinea Station, and the Star Hotel, all from the 1800s. We sure don't want anyone or anything to damage our historical sites or give them a bad name in any way and we sure don't want people to be afraid to go to any of them.

Our soldier boys from that war would be upset and turn in their graves if they knew about the disappearances and the other crazy things that have happened around here. They fought real hard for our land and to protect what was theirs. Not just them, but all of our ancestors would be upset about the way things have been. We all know that we have to do the same. We need to make things right again. We need to keep the bad folks away from our good people. We have always wanted everyone to be safe and happy. We have to keep our landmarks, our historical sites safe and make our past soldier boys proud of what our land has become. We don't want them to be ashamed of our people today. I'm just not going to let anybody corrupt our home any longer if I can help it."

"Willie? What are you up to?" asked his daddy as he stood in the doorway of their home.

"We're just out here talking about a little history daddy We think that it's time to clean up our land and keep it safe from harm."

"Well then, you can start right here in the house first because your mama says it's time for you to come in and clean up your room."

Then Russ stepped outside and said, "You can just go on in there and clean up and keep us safe from harm."

"What's that supposed to mean daddy?" Willie asked curiously.

"It means that you have too much stuff layin' around on the floor and if we're not careful, we might fall and get hurt. So, keep us safe boy!" Then he chuckled and asked Willie if he had any more questions.

"Naw daddy, I'm going right now." Then Willie looked at him very seriously and said, "But before I do go inside, I would just like to say to Rex that we'll continue our discussion a little later, because we certainly do want to take care of these matters of concern. You know how that is daddy. We don't want to leave anything just hanging without a solution. Am I right daddy? It's exactly what you taught me."

"Yeah boy, I reckon so," answered his daddy, while shaking his head as he had many times before, and feeling a little guarded after some of Willie's comments, as he had sometimes in the past, but also feeling so proud of Willie as usual.

So Willie mentioned to Rex that he'd call him in a few short minutes.

Rex said, "Sure, Willie. We'll catch up on things a little bit later. I'll wait for your call."

So then Rex waved his hand and walked towards his home. Luckily, he made it safely home without any problems. He lived only a few houses away from Willie, but it didn't stop Willie from being concerned. He always remembered that anything could happen when you glance in another direction, even for a second. He watched Rex walk home. When Rex got to his front door, Willie watched him walk into his home and called him immediately.

Russ waited for Willie to make his call. After that, he had a few things to say.

"All right Willie, what is Rex talking about? I know you're not telling me everything," said his daddy, who knew without a doubt that Willie was hiding something from him.

"I'm talking about all of the disappearances through the years and right up to a couple of weeks ago," said Willie. He still tried so hard to convince his daddy to listen and understand that he had some important points to make and some important clues to share with him.

"For the hundredth time Willie, get that stuff out of your head. What in the world am I going to do with you boy? I don't want you worrying anymore. You've changed a lot son. You're not trying to enjoy living life the way you used to. I know you're hurtin' real bad and your mama and the rest of us are hurtin' for you. Don't think about it so much Willie. You should just let us handle it."

"How can I daddy? Now, Tommy and Steve are both gone. We don't know if we'll ever see them again. They were like family to me. I can't let this go. I just can't! I believe that the police and all of us need to search each trail and everything on site at the campgrounds again. There's got to be more clues over there. You've just got to let me help look for them," said Willie, as he pleaded with his daddy, urging him to allow him to take part in the investigation and in the search for his friends.

"Willie, I can't! You searched with us the night Steve disappeared and the next day for Tommy too. You're not able to help with what they need to do now. Besides, as fast as you've had to grow up these past few years, you're still not an adult yet. You just let the police, the detectives, and all the other authorities and the other adults involved in this do the searching. We'll handle it, so don't worry Willie. We'll search every trail, every road, field, rock, and every other place in the area that we can think of until we find them. If there's anything that you kids can do to help us, we'll let you know, all right?"

"All right then daddy, I guess I don't have much choice in the matter right now, do I?"

"No, you don't right now, Willie."

"What if y'all don't find them?" asked Willie, so sadly.

"Well, we'll at least get some clues and some answers," said his daddy, trying to reassure Willie. "Nobody's going to give up looking and nobody's going to camp there again until the disappearances and the killings stop. It's a travesty and it breaks our hearts just knowing what our town has become," said his daddy, who was then trying to hold back the tears that were in his eyes.

"That's what I mean, daddy. Look at what our town has become. It's our home. We can't let this happen anymore."

"We won't, son. I promise you that we won't. We're all going to put a stop to it just as quick as we can."

Russ paced back and forth with the forlorn look he wore on his face, as he felt his tough exterior just crumble to bits and pieces. He just couldn't hold back any longer, so he lifted his hands up to his reddened face and let out a loud cry of sadness, and burst into unstoppable tears. He never wanted his children to see him this way, but little by little he felt as if he was being turned into a broken man; every time someone was reported missing. He wanted to stay strong, but he was running out of answers for his children. The disappointment they felt and the despair in their eyes was almost too much for Russ to handle. He took it very personally when it came to his family. He buried his head in his hands, so his son wouldn't see all the tears.

Willie never saw or heard his daddy cry like that before. Willie, who was trying to look and speak with confidence for his daddy's sake then said, "Daddy, don't worry. We're all going to pull ourselves together and make things better. We've all shed tears and now it's time for nothing but happiness. Maybe Tommy and Steve will be found safe 'n' sound and everything will be all right again."

Rae Ann knew what happened that day, because Willie had confided in her. Now, she briefly forgot about her physical pain because she was overcome by her emotional pain, when remembering her cousin's sadness and sincerity. She thought to herself . . . Willie had the best attitude back then, and he still does today. I just know that wherever he is, he's fine. I have nothing but fond memories of my cousin; she felt it in her heart as she reminisced once more. But where is my cousin now? Where is that optimism of his now?

Rae Ann felt that she could certainly use some of Willie's optimism right now.

She thought to herself—I wish I could see you now cousin. Those things happened so long ago, but they're still so very real today.

After every killing, it was as if a part of each one of us died, too, but we all vowed that it will end and the haunting will be over. I can't bare for this to go on much longer. Our families should be able to live the way they want to live and feel what they really want to feel.

CHAPTER 14

As more years passed, the attitudes and personalities of the wonderful down-home communities became more somber, and subdued as sadness enveloped the families. The ambiance in the town took over like an unleashed wild weapon, striking the unsuspecting ones at its every whim. The wooded areas were still forbidden to all because anyone who entered was still in danger of falling into the sneaky clasp of the vicious, unknown killer. It still wasn't known as to whether or not there was one, or more than one killer.

There was a reported number of at least seventeen more missing persons and at least seven more deaths and it was believed that each of these cases were all linked together.

Families moved away. Some families moved together to form safety in numbers. Country life as they knew it had drastically changed. There was once a time when life consisted of simple living with simple pleasures, freely moving about; but now, a watchful eye was kept, constant guard from mounting suspicion, going out only when there was a need to. It was as if there was an adverse effect for living life with pleasure. It was because that's when the abductions seem to happen. So this extreme precaution became a part of everyday living for a lot of the towns people. Their past experiences taught them to always stay on constant guard, especially if it involved children.

Finally, about ten or so years later, the time came when the number of crimes decreased and once again as in previous years, people actually started to feel like things were going to be all right again. Rae Ann remembered that it was then that they could actually smile again, without looking behind, without digging up the past; at least for a while.

Rae Ann, her cousins, and some friends, decided to go out. They weren't going to let these incidents destroy their entire lives. They refused to permit anyone to drain their lives of any pleasure that existed for them any longer. They wanted to enjoy and appreciate every minute they had together. With this new outlook on life, and with their unbroken spirits, they went out; the way they used to.

Rae Ann remembered one particular time, in her twenties. It was another experience that none of them would ever forget. The close relationships that their family shared together within their community were stronger than ever. The evening started out to be one of the best times that they ever had together.

This is how Rae Ann remembered that night—a few of her cousins and she got together and drove to the *Rustle Up Karaoke Dance Hall and Lounge.* Rae Ann, Willie, Ray, Junior, Charles, Billy, a friend of theirs named Jenny, and another friend whose name was Blair, and cousin Francis, Sue, and Dawn walked inside and found a booth near the stage and ordered a pitcher of cold beer.

Someone was already up on stage singin' *Your Cheatin' Heart,* which was one of their favorite songs.

Charles said, "This is definitely our night."

Willie said, "Oh yeah boy, that's for sure 'cause they're already singin' and playin' our song."

"Yeah, said Rae Ann, "That's been our song ever since granddaddy taught us all how to sing and play it on his guitar when we were children."

Sue said, "This night is already off to a great start, and it can only keep gettin' better!"

Cousin Junior chimed in, "This place is really jumpin' and I can hardly wait to get on that dance floor." So Junior made his way through the crowd, and found a girl to dance with. They found a spot and joined in with everyone else who was dancing and singing along with the guy performing on stage.

The cousins were ecstatic to all be together again. The morale was high and the adrenalin was climbin' high. No one could hold a candle to the happiness that was shared that night.

Willie raised his glass and said, "When times get bad, there's no excuse for cheatin' 'cause all a man needs is one good, faithful woman."

Rae Ann then commented, "Or one good faithful man, and then you have it all." They all held their beer mugs up high and drank.

Rae Ann said, "Let's all promise that we will always be the best husband or wife, boyfriend or girlfriend that we can possibly be and if something's wrong, we'll discuss it and try to work it out instead of going out somewhere to do something stupid that we'll regret later. Now let's drink to that."

"This is what life is all about. Close families and good friendships, good clean living, some pleasure, and nothing's better than having a great relationship with the one you love."

Then they all clicked their beer mugs together and drank a little more to that, too.

"Now, with all this drinkin' we're doin' tonight, we all have to remember our rule—nobody can leave here until they're sober."

"That's right. We're all stickin' to that rule," said Dawn, "but right now, let's have some fun."

Willie said, "Hey Rae Ann, let's go up on stage and sing a song or two in front of everybody here. Come on now, girl."

"All right, let's show 'em what we got. I think they'll enjoy our songs tonight."

They knew most of the crowd at the bar. Some, they had known all of their lives. They all continued to be a *close-knit* community in Caroline through the years, and they felt comfortable enough to sing in front of everyone.

Willie went outside and got his guitar out of his car. When he came back, he whispered to Rae Ann "Hey girl, I've got to talk to you after we finish up with our song." Rae Ann answered "Will do cousin."

"Why don't we sing a song by Johnny Cash?"

"You got it, Rae Ann!"

"Okay folks, we want all of y'all to sing with us and get on that dance floor and dance!"

Willie started playing his guitar and the excited crowd went wild. They couldn't have picked a better night to get together. Everyone clapped their hands and they danced and sang. The night was perfect. They were finally able to relax. Nothing could go wrong, **or could it?**

Today, as Rae Ann remembered that night long ago, she had a gut feeling—back then, that something could happen. She continued to remember that night.

When Willie first arrived at the lounge that night, he noticed that one of the trucks in the parking lot looked like Randy's old pickup truck. He hadn't given that guy any thought for a long time now. Willie hoped that ol' bully from childhood wasn't back in town. He still believed that Randy had a lot to do with young Mike, who disappeared years ago. Willie never forgot that they broke into his aunt's home, and that Randy fooled everyone, into believing that Mike just disappeared. He didn't want to believe that it was Randy's truck, so he didn't mention it to anyone, but when he went outside to get his guitar, he took a closer look at the truck. That truck belonged to Randy's family. When he saw the license plates, he knew it was Randy's old truck. He mentioned it to Rae Ann, and even though it meant Randy was probably there, they didn't want anyone to feel alarmed since they saw no signs of him. Shortly after Willie told Rae Ann, they headed back to their booth.

Sue's voice was heard clear across the dance floor and she sounded agitated with someone, so they all got up and walked over to where she was, and their tempers flared. Randy was there, trying to make Sue dance with him and he was singing, grabbing at her and pulling her close to him, swaying her from side to side along with him. They could hear him humming and singing a song that he obviously made up himself. He was singing words like—*come a little closer; dance a little dance; sing a little song; dance with me baby; all night long.*

Willie shouted, "Hey let her go!"

Randy answered, "Mind your own business. We're dancin,' and I'm singin' a little song to Sue."

Then Randy turned around and saw Rae Ann and exclaimed "Hey Rae Ann. It's been a long time since I've seen your pretty face. Come on and dance with me since your sister is just as stubborn as she always was. I can't get her to loosen up for me." He said this with a condescending tone in his voice.

"Not on your life, you ol' dirt bag," answered Rae Ann with a look of disgust on her face. "I wouldn't dance with you if my life depended on it and you don't know how to sing anyway. That wasn't a song comin' out of your mouth. That was just pure crap! Besides, you stink too much. No one wants to be around someone like you; somebody that just plain stinks more than anyone or anything imaginable."

"Rae Ann's right," said her sister Sue. "Why are you even back here in town?"

Then Randy let go of Sue and lifted his arm as if he was going to hit her, but he stopped and put his hands to his sides and said, "You just go on and walk back over there where they are. I'm just about finished with you anyway." Then he looked at the others. He decided that he had more to say to them.

"First of all, I think you better mind your manners. Y'all always thought y'all were too good for me and my family, but someday, you'll find out that none of you are any better . . . me or my family. I thought I'd come back and visit some old friends of mine tonight. It's a coincidence that y'all are here on the same night as me. Believe me, there are folks that want to be around me. They try to look past my so-called faults that y'all think I have. I would think that you'd be a little more courteous to me. After all, it's been a long time since I've seen any of you. I haven't seen you folks since our school days."

Willie then said, "It still ain't been long enough."

"You don't have to act like that Willie. Don't you think you're being a little snide?" Randy asked with a gruff tone in his voice. A little shrimp like you ain't got a chance around a man like me."

Willie looked at him fiercely and responded by saying, "I'd be more than snide to you if I had things my way, so don't even try to provoke me. You didn't know how to act like a normal boy during your childhood, so you sure don't know how to act like a man now. We tried to get along with you, but you turned out to be a big troublemaker, so we didn't want anything to do with you back then and we don't want anything to do with you now."

"Anyway, Willie isn't being snide, Randy, he's just being truthful." Rae Ann, looking directly into Randy's brown eyes, then said, "If you don't like the way that you're being treated, then why don't you just go find another bar to hang out at tonight? It's obvious that you're not welcome here. You could make this a good night for yourself and for the rest of us too, if you'd just leave."

"Well, I just might let you all have your way tonight. I'll go somewhere else for now, but I guarantee that I'll catch up with y'all later—especially, with the two of you, Rae Ann. Did you hear what I just told your cousin, Willie?"

"Yeah, I heard you, but don't count on catching up with us Randy; not if we have anything to do with it."

"Oh, you can count on it all right." Then Randy walked past Rae Ann and the others that were standing around together, but not without shoving Willie into the wall behind them first. Then Randy said, "I'll be seeing ya."

Willie didn't lose his temper at that point though. Instead, he just stared at Randy until Randy was out of sight. Willie was starting to feel concern for his own well-being and for the others though. Some of his old suspicions and fears were starting to surface again. He was determined that he wasn't going to let this run-in with Randy ruin their night. So they all went back to their booth and sat down. Willie thought he better take his guitar back to the car, so he stood back up and said, "I'll be back in a minute or two y'all."

"Willie, do you think we should go out there with you?" asked Junior.

"Naw, I think I'll be fine. It'll just take me a minute." Then he picked up his guitar and went out the door.

The others didn't really feel comfortable about Willie going out there alone, but they stayed right where they were since that was what he wanted.

So about fifteen minutes went by and they noticed that he hadn't returned yet, so they were concerned and went outside to find out what was taking him so long to get back inside. When they walked outside, they saw and heard Willie and Randy having a heated discussion. They could hear Randy asking Willie if he remembered what he had said inside the bar and Willie telling him that he remembered every word. Randy told him that he was goin' to teach him a lesson. He said that he was going to bring the Matthews family, their friends, and their kin down to his level. Willie did start to lose his temper and yelled, "Randy, why don't you just get the hell out of here? What the hell is wrong with you? You had lots of chances to straighten yourself out, but you didn't want to. You brought it all on yourself. Now get the hell out of here and leave decent folks alone. You don't belong here anymore." Then Willie started to swing his fist into Randy's mouth, but Junior and Charles ran up to him and stopped him before he could hit Randy.

"Why did y'all stop me?"

Charles said, "'cause we don't want any more trouble tonight. It's no tellin' what Randy would have done if you punched him. It takes a lot of guts for you to avoid hittin' him."

"You're right. Thanks for stopping me. Charles, why is that lunatic back in town? You know he didn't come here just to visit some of his friends." Then Willie picked his guitar off the ground and put it in his trunk.

"I don't know Willie, but you need to be careful. I don't think you should go anywhere alone tonight."

"What? Let him think that I'm scared of him? No way! All I know is that he better get the hell out of this town quick, 'cause we're not going to put up with it. Hey, I'll see y'all a little later. I'm going to get home now. That bully's ruined everything tonight, so I'm going home. I'll call you when I get there," said Willie.

"Okay, be careful Willie and don't worry about anything. We'll talk things out tomorrow and figure out what we're all going to do about him."

"Okay, that sounds good. An even better idea would be for the sheriff to find a reason to lock his tail up. That shouldn't be hard to do."

Then he got into his car and left. Rae Ann and the others, left about half an hour later. They drove on the same road, heading back to their homes. Suddenly, they pulled over to the side of the road and they saw Willie's car and just a few feet away from the car was Willie, lying down on the side of the road. He had been beaten up. Dawn called an ambulance and soon afterward, Willie woke up in a hospital room. He couldn't remember anything much except that there was a fairly large tree branch on the road, so he had to stop his car and he got out to move it off the road. The next thing he remembered was that someone jumped him from behind and now, here he is, in the hospital, all bandaged up and in a lot of pain.

He looked around him and saw a lot of friends and family surrounding him. He looked at them with a grin and said, "You'd think I had died or something. It's right many of y'all here. I love y'all too, but can you folks give me a little bit of breathing room?" They all laughed. Then he said, "I feel like crap."

"Well, I bet you do, but you sure sound like yourself and that's a good sign," said Francis.

"Willie, do you think Randy might have jumped you tonight? We all know that he's too cowardly to take responsibility for any wrong doing," said Charles.

"Seeing you just lying there on the road scared us Willie. Thank goodness you're going to be all right."

"Yeah, Randy really messed up our good time tonight. I'm going to make sure that I tell the police about how much trouble Randy 'causes for people and how dangerous we think he is. Maybe I'll get lucky and they'll listen to me for once."

Willie believed that Randy had attacked him, but he couldn't see what the person looked like, so he was uncertain that he could prove anything. That always seemed to be the case. They've never been able to prove anything against Randy.

"Well . . . Willie, the police and a detective are going to talk to you anyway," said Dawn.

"Okay, Dawn, I'm ready to talk to them," said Willie.

"All right Willie, I'm going home now, but don't you even think about leavin' this hospital alone once you're discharged," said Dawn, and then she continues telling him, "and don't you dare even try to leave this hospital before you're discharged either. One of us will take you home. All right Willie?"

"All right, Dawn."

Dawn then said, "No one's told mama or daddy about what happened to you tonight. None of us told them about Randy being back in town either. We don't want to upset them."

"That's good Dawn. There's no reason for them to know about this. Hopefully, Randy will be long gone by tomorrow."

"Okay, here come the police now, so we're all going to go, 'cause we know that you're going to be just fine and we'll see you first thing in the morning."

Then they gave him a hug and left for the night.

Willie could hardly wait to talk to the police, because he wanted to tell them everything that he could about Randy. He wasn't sure if they would think everything was as relevant as he did, but he wanted to tell them anyway, just in case the information would be useful. He thought they'd at least take some notes. He hoped that they would pick Randy up and take him to jail.

Rae Ann never forgot that night. As far as she was concerned, it was just more proof that Randy was involved in all of this somehow. If Randy was the murderer and kidnapper, she knew that he'd be caught up with someday. Willie was lucky that he wasn't kidnapped or killed that night. Maybe Randy realized that if he had killed Willie, or even kidnapped him, he'd easily be caught and quickly too. Rae Ann was certain of that. It was unfortunate that he wasn't arrested for what happened to Willie. The police decided that there wasn't enough proof again. Rae Ann thought to herself—someday it'll happen. Randy will be out of our lives forever.

CHAPTER 15

As far as Rae Ann and her family and their relatives knew, Randy had disappeared once again. After that night, no one saw him for many years, but they did hear about more strange occurrences and crimes in Caroline, and in some areas nearby.

Rae Ann's sister, Sue, got married. She and her husband even moved away. Her husband wanted Sue out of harm's way. He said they'd move back when things were back to normal again. That could take an entire lifetime. Sue wasn't happy about it, but she loved her husband and stood by his decision. They did call often and visited too, but one morning her husband came to Bowling Green to buy some wood. Sue was visiting some of their friends at that time. The wood in town could be purchased at a better price, so he told Sue he'd be back in a couple of hours, but he was never seen again. Sue's heart was broken and it ached for her husband. Sue ended up moving back to Caroline County. She didn't think anyone was safe anywhere, so it no longer mattered where she lived. She lost her zest for life and never quite recovered emotionally from her loss. There are no words or emotions that could express or describe the anger or the sadness that Sue felt.

Others got married, including Rae Ann. She was married and divorced within four years and has two beautiful daughters who are young women now. Time just felt like it flew by once she became a mother. Most of her cousins either married or remarried, except for Little Willie. He was still quite a handful. It would be quite a challenge for any woman to tie him down. A committed relationship just didn't seem to be part of his vocabulary. Everyone loved Willie, though. He turned out to be a fine and decent, intelligent, and caring young man.

Rae Ann had the same feelings and opinions and drew some of the same conclusions today, as in past years. She began to think and feel without a doubt, that there was a connection between all that happened in the past and all that's happening now. She knew now that she wouldn't give up on doing all she could to stay alive. She was determined to live long enough to make sure that justice would be done. He deserved everything that he had coming to him if he's still living. He just couldn't get away any longer without being punished for his crimes. She wanted to make sure everyone knew what kind of person he really is or was—whatever the case may be. Could Randy be the dirt man? Well, whoever the dirt man is didn't matter right now. All that matters is that he is caught and hopefully, he'll experience a lot of the pain that his victims had. It would be quite an accomplishment for her or Willie to be the one to put a stop to the killings. It would be a wonderful thing for the folks in their community to have no more worries and it would definitely bring some closure for a lot of the families.

Rae Ann still wanted to know what happened to Randy; just for her piece of mind. It was believed by most that Randy finally met his match. Maybe no one heard from him or saw him again because he died or maybe he finally got locked up. No one could believe that he had turned his life around. They all felt that he was just too mean and he didn't want to make any good changes in his life.

During the years that Randy was out of sight, Rae Ann and the others actually enjoyed living their lives again.

Some of those unforgettable times, were still branded in their memories.

Here today, still stuck here in this murky, dirty, water, she could remember back to a time when things weren't going well again.

Rae Ann vaguely remembered another turbulent time when she learned of a very serious illness she had, and kept it a secret from her daughters, and from her relatives. Only the doctors and her specialists knew. Right now, she couldn't even recall what the name of the illness is. She remembered that she swore them to secrecy. That was the only way that she would follow the instructions of the fine, outstanding physicians.

Rae Ann was remembering, and thinking to herself again . . . I remember when I planned to take my daughters out for a delicious lunch at one of our favorite restaurants. I hadn't quite decided if I was going to tell them how ill I am. I didn't want anything to change in our relationships. I wanted to continue living the way I had always lived my life. I did know however, that I wanted to spend as much time with them as I could before I made any kind of decisions. So we met up with each other at my house and we took my car. I was well enough to drive, so I did. We had the radio on and we were singing and joking around and giggling like little school children, when all of a sudden; a car came out of almost nowhere and tried to force us off the road. She began to remember that day as if it just happened minutes ago, even the exact words that were exchanged between them. What she recalled was . . .

"Heather? Trish? Your seat belts are on tight, right? Uhhh . . . oh no!" Rae Ann screamed.

"Whoa . . . mama!!!" screamed the girls.

We swerved from one side of the mountainous road to the other and spun around, but I had a good grip on the steering wheel. I gained control, but not before first going off the road into a ridged ditch just before we reached the steep embankment. The car was tilted to one side, but not enough for it to overturn. I could see from the car windows. There was a long stretch of the rocky mountainside, rolling out for miles down the embankment. We missed sliding down the mountainside only by a few feet. I cried out to my girls, "Are y'all all right? I want to hear your voices." They both answered and we still managed to hug each other, even in the awkward positions we were in, from being knocked around and swung to one side in the car; even with our seat-belts on; although they were twisted and loosened from the movements. They were lucky that the seat-belts didn't snap in half. The other driver didn't even stop to help and wasn't anywhere in sight. Fortunately, someone did see us and called an ambulance. We decided that we should go to the hospital. The police did their usual report and then we rode inside the ambulance to the hospital.

Once we arrived, we were separated and taken to our individual rooms for examination. Heather was told that she would be one of the first to be seen since she had problems with her ankle. They took me right away, too. They rushed me to another wing of the hospital. I learned later that Trish was seen after Heather was examined.

Heather got examined by a very tall, handsome doctor with crystal blue-colored eyes and dark brown hair. He looked very strong, but had a very gentle way with her. She thought it was love at first sight. As far as she was concerned, the good Dr. Aaron Stevens could keep her in his care for the remainder of her lifetime because she already believed that he was the man of her dreams. Although Heather hoped that she was in perfect health, she anticipated seeing Dr. Stevens many more times. Hopefully, he'd see her not only as his patient, but as someone that he would like to have a personal, long-lasting, intimate relationship with, now and in his future. She wondered if he felt that "little spark" that she felt as soon as she met him.

Dr. Stevens came into the room. He checked her ankle for swelling and pain and called in his nurse. X-Rays were also taken. Then the nurse left the room after reading the chart.

Heather asked, "Dr. Stevens, Am I going to be all right? How are Trisha and my mother doing? Are they going to be all right?"

Dr. Stevens looked at her with a sincere smile and answered softly, telling her that she was in perfect shape as far as he could see but that he was waiting for a couple more test results, and then he'd know for sure.

"Your sister is just about ready to be examined by me, so after I'm done, I'll find out if your test results are ready, and then I should be ready to talk to you about your health, Miss Miles."

"Well doc, why don't you just call me by my first name? It's Heather."

"Okay Heather, and when we're not around my colleagues, you can call me Aaron unless you prefer to call me doc."

"It'll be my pleasure, doc. Then Heather looked concerned as she asked, "How is our mother doing Aaron?"

"Your mother is being seen by Dr. Hinson and Dr. Tomlin, who are some of the finest doctors that we have on staff here at the hospital. They're very qualified and she's in excellent hands. Her injuries appear to be a little more extensive than yours or Trisha's injuries, but don't worry. All right, now I have to go examine your sister."

"I'll wait for you Aaron," Heather whispered to him in an alluring voice, while wearing a big smile, engaging him with her big, wide green eyes, while trying to entice him with her feminine charm as he walked past her on his way out, hopefully just enough for him to become intrigued and interested.

He was mesmerized by her beauty, but he wanted to stay focused while at work.

On the way out, Aaron said, "It's going to be a long day for your family. There are vending machines and the cafeteria's opened if you'd like anything to eat. The food is actually pretty tasty. I should be done in about an hour, so I can meet you there or in the waiting area near your mother's room."

"I'll go to the cafeteria. I'm pretty hungry. We were on our way to one of our favorite restaurants right before the accident. Have you ever heard of the Down Home Fixin's Diner? They fix the best pork chops smothered in gravy that anyone's ever eaten. They've won competitions for their great food. We'll just have to go another time. Hospital food will have to do for now. After I eat, I'll go to the waiting area," said Heather.

"All right, I'll meet you there in about an hour then," said Aaron. Oh, and by the way . . . I have eaten at the Down Home Fixins' Diner and the food is great, but I could give them a run for their money in the smothered pork chop category."

"You're funny, doc. You are kidding though right? You don't even look like the type of person that would cook some real southern food like smothered pork chops."

"No, I kid you not. Don't let my appearance fool you. I'm as southern as they come.*"*

"Well, I'll have to put you to the test. It'll be me against you in a food competition. The loser will have to go wherever the winner wants to go for an entire night."

"You're on! I accept the challenge! This competition will be very entertaining. I'll let you know where we're going to go as soon as I give it plenty of thought, and have a day or two of free time that I can squeeze in; since we can assume that I'm going to win the competition."

"You'll let me know? You're just being funny again right doc? I can say for now that we can have the competition at my house, and we have to go dancin' when I win. How does that sound?"

"Just being funny again? You wish. You're going to find out that I my cooking can make your mouth water because it's so delicious, Heather."

"Aaron, thank you so much for your kindness. I feel so much better knowing that we're in your care."

"It's my pleasure," he answered as he looked at her fondly. "Okay, I really do have to go examine your sister now."

"Aaron, will you let her know where I'll be?"

"I will let her know." Then while still looking at her, he went out the door to the examining room where Heather's sister Trisha was waiting for him.

Heather could not believe what just happened between her and Dr. Aaron Stevens. She really believed that it was a new relationship that was meant to be. She hoped he would feel the same way about her.

"Hello, Mrs. Gregory, I'm Dr. Aaron Stevens. I'm going to examine you now."

"Hello, Dr. Stevens. Have you examined my sister or my mother yet?"

"Yes, I examined your sister. As a matter of fact, I just left from there."

"Oh, uh huh, now I know why I've been waiting here a little longer than I expected. Heather wouldn't let you out of her room would she?"

Aaron didn't quite know how to answer that question, so he hesitated for a moment and then could only reply, "Uh, well," as he fumbled through the papers. It was apparent that he was at a loss of words but he was grinning from ear to ear.

Then Trish laughed and said, "Don't bother answering my question, Dr. Stevens, 'cause the look on your face explains everything." Then Trisha laughed again and said, "Relax Dr. Stevens. I'm just having a little fun."

"Well, actually, your sister and I have made some plans."

"I think it's just wonderful," said Trisha. "Heather really does like you then. I can see that you're definitely her type."

"Well, now let's see how you're doing physically. I can certainly tell that you're resilient and that you're feeling happy, even after the terrible accident, so you must not be in any extreme physical pain. I see you have some nasty bruises and there's a cut on your forehead, but you won't need any stitches. Did you feel any type of pain when you laughed a few moments ago, Mrs. Gregory?"

"Nope, doctor . . . none at all," answered Trisha. "Since, you and our family are on a more personal level now, you can call me Trisha or Trish if you'd like."

"All right, thank you," said Aaron. "You and Heather can call me by my first name, Aaron, when my colleagues aren't around."

"Thank you Aaron. I'll do that and I'm sure that Heather will too."

Aaron said, "She already does. By the way, Heather's in the cafeteria right now and in a little less than an hour from now, she'll be in the waiting area near your mother's room. After I finish examining you, and after I get Heather's and your results back, I'll meet with the two of you there."

"Will do," said Trisha. "Thanks for the info."

"You're quite welcome. I think the two of you are going to be just fine."

"I hope so," said Trisha. "I have to call my husband and let him know just as soon as possible, too. He couldn't be here because he's in the military and stationed outside of Virginia right now. I'm just glad that he hasn't been deployed yet. When he's here, I stay with him in military housing. Since he's away, I've been spending some nights at Heather's house, near mama's house. Aaron, will you speak with him as a favor to me, so he can hear it straight from you that I'm okay? I know he worries and he knows that I might not tell him right away if anything was seriously wrong with me. I don't like keeping anything from him, but he has so many responsibilities, so sometimes I just wait a little longer than he prefers. I just don't want him to be upset about anything."

"Well, let's find out what the results are first, okay Trish? We don't want to assume the worst before we really know. I will talk to him if you'd like for me to, though."

"That's good. At least he won't be concerned then," said Trish. She agreed to wait until they got the final test results.

"What about our mother?"

"Don't worry because as I told your sister, we have two very well-known, very qualified specialists, who are also two of the best here at the hospital. She's in excellent hands." He knew he had to choose his words very carefully because of HIPPA privacy, the code of ethics, and also because of a promise that he made to their mother.

"Why does she have to see specialists?"

"Well, we don't want to take any chances. We want to do all we can for her. The accident has really taken a toll on her and there are other various factors to consider, such as her age. It's better that you speak with her."

After finishing up with Trisha, he let her know that he had two more patients to check on.

"All right Trish, I'll meet up with the two of you in the cafeteria or in the waiting room within an hour or so. Will you let your sister know that I might be delayed a little longer than I first expected?"

"Sure Aaron. By the way, thanks for everything."

"You're welcome. Now please don't worry about the tests. You ladies don't need any additional stress to this difficult day the two of you have had. I certainly hope y'all don't have any more problems with anyone on the road anymore."

"Yeah, it's strange the way the accident happened. We've never experienced anything quite like that before."

"I can assure you that it doesn't usually take the police around here long to catch hit-and-run criminals. Well, enjoy your meal and I'll see you ladies shortly."

"Oh, I'll enjoy my meal because I'm starving. I could eat just about anything in sight right now. See ya, Aaron. Good luck with your other patients."

Doctor Aaron Stevens then went on his way down the hall and out of Trisha's sight. Then Trisha took the elevator to the hospital cafeteria and found Heather sitting there with enough food on the table for three people.

"Hi sis! Are you just a little bit hungry? The food must not be that bad. It's enough here to feed the military."

"It's not bad at all," said Heather.

"Well, then let me try some. Hmmm, this looks good and cheesy," said Trish, as she grabbed a bite-size piece of a cheesy french fry from Heather's plate.

"It's really good isn't it?" Then Trish grabbed another one.

"Hey, hands off. Get your own Trish! There's plenty more over there that you can buy."

"Okay, I will, right after I get one more from your plate." Heather then tried to pull her plate from under Trisha's hand, but couldn't do it fast enough. They looked at each other and smiled.

"Seriously now, we need to talk about mama," said Trish.

"Yeah, we do."

So Trish got her food and sat across from Heather. "I think there's something wrong with mama."

"Why Trish?"

"Because more doctors have examined her than us and they're still up there with her, running more tests. Have you noticed that they've been up there for quite a while now? It didn't take even half the time for us to be examined as it has for her."

Heather then reminded her, that the doctors were checking on other patients too. "If there's anything seriously wrong with mama, she'll tell us, when she's ready to tell us."

"Yeah, I guess so, sooner or later right?"

"Trish, don't worry. We have to *think positive*, so let's be happy that the three of us are alive and here together."

"Okay, but I still think mama's hiding something."

"Well, so do I. We'll find out more from the doctors."

"Speaking of doctors . . . Dr. Stevens is very good-looking with his blue eyes and dark brown hair and he's so friendly."

"Yeah, he's very handsome and I just want to jump and dive right into those blue eyes. It would be like jumping into a pool of water. Better yet, a girl just might want to dive right into his arms."

"Okay, Heather. I already know that you and Aaron have made plans, so you can save your diving skills for later and concentrate on mama for now. All right?"

"All right, but let me remind you that you brought the whole subject of our good doctor up."

"Woo hoo, speaking of our good doctor . . . here he comes right now," said Trish.

Doctor Stevens walked over to their table and asked Heather if he could speak with her alone for a moment or two. Heather then got up with a slightly curious look on her face. She wondered if there was any reason to worry. "What is it Dr. Stevens? I mean Aaron."

"Don't worry. I just wanted to tell you that your mother informed me that we cannot further examine her unless I promise to at least have coffee with you today. She's very upbeat, and has a good sense of humor; considering what she's been through. I was going to tell her that we already made plans, but she didn't give me a chance. So now, you and I need to make plans to have coffee together, as soon as I can free up some time."

"I'm sorry Aaron. My mother is very strong-willed, and overly protective, and she's used to having her way most of the time. I don't expect for you to have coffee with me simply because she wants us to."

"I wouldn't do it for that reason. I already told her that I would have coffee with you. It'll give us another chance to get to know each other. I also want to mention that she's already informed me that she'd like two grandchildren, so since I'm practically family—well, when we have coffee, you can tell me what some of your secret ingredients in your smothered pork chops."

"Aaron, you're so funny, I'd love to, but I'm not going to tell you what the secret ingredients are."

Heather and Aaron could hardly keep from laughing. Then he reached for her hand and gave it a slight squeeze and let go. He looked forward to their first date.

She was so happy that he took her by her hand. She was already thinking about their dates ahead. Her mama had no idea that she and Aaron had made plans together, even before her mama got involved.

"Just wait until I tell mama that we already made a date. She probably won't ever learn to stop meddling. I know she meant well though. She'll be one proud mama once she finds out."

"I'm sure she will be."

He looked at the time. Then he looked at Heather.

"I have to go speak with Dr. Hinson and Dr. Tomlin for a few minutes," said Aaron.

"Well, Trish and I are just about ready to head over to the waiting area, so we'll meet you there shortly if that's okay. Trish wants to finish her dinner first, so it'll be a few more minutes."

"Yes, that would be a perfect time. I'm going up there right now, so by the time you ladies come up, we'll talk about the tests." Then Aaron left once again.

"Hey Heather, maybe I have been worrying for nothing," said Trish with a sigh of relief. It might not be anything seriously wrong with mama. She's still as spirited as ever, playing matchmaker and everything.

"Yeah, mama is still trying to take care of us, Trish." They looked at each other and giggled a little bit.

Heather smiled and said, "Mama can take care of me like this anytime she wants to, because now, thanks to her, I don't have just one date with Aaron, but I have two dates."

Trish grinned and said, "You are a spoiled little woman, sis."

In the waiting area, it started to feel like they were there for eternity. Down the hallway, Dr. Stevens and the other two doctors were standing in the doorway of their mother's room, and they appeared to be in deep discussion.

"What do you think they're saying about mama Trish?" asked Heather with concern.

"I'm not sure, but I'm starting to worry again."

"Me too," said Heather. "This just doesn't feel right. Why haven't they released mama yet?"

"I don't know. We need to just think positive and be patient."

"Yeah, but you know that they can't tell us anything that she doesn't want us to know."

"Right; nothing until she's *good 'n' ready*."

"Yeah, when it's convenient for her."

"Don't be so hard on mama. She just don't want us to worry or be upset about anything."

Heather sighed. "That's for sure Trish, but maybe if we approach them and speak to them about our concerns, they'll consider telling us more than they've told us so far. I know that mama hasn't been feeling very well lately."

"I know, but forget it. We've tried our persuasive tactics before, and it's never worked. It was a good thought though sis."

CHAPTER 16

I'm glad that my daughters and Aaron told me all about their conversations at the hospital, and about the sparks that flew between Aaron and Heather. That kind of genuine attraction is rare. I'm glad that something good came out of that long, exhausting day at the hospital. I remember that day pretty well now. I remember Heather and Aaron dated for a few months after that, too, and that they got married.

I still don't know why that accident happened back then. I don't know if there is any connection between that accident and why I'm here today. I still can't even remember how I got here. I know that one day, I'll be able to figure everything out.

It was difficult to convince my daughters that the doctors had to take more time to examine people my age. My daughters were right. I wasn't going to let the doctors tell them anything that I didn't want them to know. I wasn't ready to tell them anything at all about my condition yet. I wasn't ready to tell them about some of the physical pain I was in sometimes. The time just wasn't right. I'm comfortable with that decision and I felt that I made the right decision then. I still can't remember exactly what my final diagnosis or my prognosis was. I am pretty certain that there is something seriously wrong with my health. These bits and pieces of my memory are really starting to annoy me. This is just too much of an unsolved puzzle for me right now. If I could only remember more. Is this the price that I have to pay for keeping my illness a secret from them? Now, it's even a secret from me.

I know I had reasons for not telling them, and I hope they'll both understand. At least I know that their lives will be fine. I am the proud grandma of a little boy that Trish gave birth to. My grandma and granddaddy were there for both weddings. They were so happy and acted a lot like newlyweds themselves, as they smiled and danced together at both weddings. We can only admire people like them who remain strong in their relationships as married couples.

Rae Ann thought more about how their lives had changed. She wasn't sure if the good things in her life really would outweigh the bad in her life that's seemingly plagued by discontentment. Everyone she loves has been tormented over the haunting memories. She knew that she didn't want to live like this any longer.

Something has to happen soon. There just had to be an end to this emotional turmoil.

Rae Ann felt so lonely right now. There was still no sign of anyone by the river. Another time that she felt this lonely, was when her grandparents died. It was one of the most difficult times for Rae Ann and the rest of the family. When her grandparents passed away, she could barely face her personal loss. Rae Ann misses them just as much today as the day she first learned the sad news. Luckily, they both died of natural causes. She never thought about living life without them. She never wanted to find out, but she knew then and now, that it's another one of the harsh realities of life that we all have to experience some time or another.

It was a very lonely time for all of them. For Rae Ann, it felt all so unfair—*she just felt so alone.* How could she just keep losing everyone who was so close and so dear to her? She felt like she had no one at all. Although her daughters were still a big part of her life, they had their own families. Most of her relatives and friends all had their own families. Others, that she was once close to, had moved away, or were friends that had mysteriously disappeared through the years.

She thought about the age differences between her grandma and granddaddy and some of their friends. Some of them were so much older than they were. She looked at the Johnsons, in their nineties, and they're still living. Grandma and granddaddy lived good, clean, decent lives. Why did they die first? A brief moment of envy escalated inside her. It hurt so much because she knew she couldn't have her grandparents back. She couldn't look forward to seeing them almost every day; the way she used to. How could she not feel a little bit jealous? She had known them since she was a child and they were some of her grandparents' closest friends. She started to feel a little guilty about the thoughts that raced through her mind, but she knew that these emotions racing inside her would soon pass.

Rae Ann hated the thought of the changes that would come about in her life. There was a void inside her heart that she knew could never be filled. She felt so sick inside. She could barely get through her grandfather's funeral and she wondered how she could possibly get through her grandma's funeral that day—*but she did, just like everyone else.* Her grandparents, so wisely told her, her sister, and brother, to stay strong; because no matter how tough things got, they could always get through anything together, because they all loved each other. They endured many challenges in their lives through the years and although it was very tough for them, but they remained strong, just as they were taught to do.

Rae Ann only appeared to cope with her loss, but in actuality, she didn't feel or show much emotion anymore. She wanted to do what was expected of her. She wondered how she could have a good life without the people that she loved so much. She questioned if there was any way at all that her life could ever improve for the better, or if this is simply the way it was going to be from now on. Could she ever be truly happy again?

Today, her frail, thin body just laid there, afloat, moving with the current of the river water. Now, her head just hung with her cheek in the water, along with one of her legs flip-flopping in the water, as the water swished around. Could things get any worse than they are now? Could they get worse than she could ever imagine? Would she die right here?

She could see a bird with large flowing wings that had nestled itself down on the water near her. It stared into Rae Ann's eyes. Then, she could feel and see movement beneath one of her feet. She just hoped it wasn't a snake in the water. Something squiggled around as the bird reached for it and caught it in its beak. Then the bird was still for a few moments. Rae Ann decided to speak to the bird, saying, "Well, just don't stare at me. Put yourself to good use and find some help. If I'm rescued, I'll catch a fish for you. Shoot! I'll catch fifty fish for you. Oh, I would like to be like you and take my wings and fly anywhere I want; to some of the most beautiful places on earth, but I guess I'm not goin' anywhere. I guess there's nothing you can do for me, so why don't you just fly away? Just get the hell away from me."

She didn't mean it. She still loved birds and everything about nature. She just wanted to leave and live as freely as the bird could.

The tears streamed down her cheeks. Rae Ann wasn't aware that love was all around her, even though some of her loved ones are no longer here. In her heart and in her mind, she still wanted her life to be filled with zest. She still had the yearning for her life to be good again, but was this desire enough?

The water got colder, but there was nothing that she could do. There was still no one in sight, who could help her. Rae Ann was unaware that her cousin, Willie had just arrived in town.

CHAPTER 17

"Here we are Willie, back at home and now it's ours together! I can hardly wait to go inside. I'm so excited! Do you think you're going to miss being a single man?" asked Terry Lynn.

"No, there's not even a little chance of that," replied Willie. "We're meant to be together. That's all there is to it."

"Yeah, it's our destiny, Willie. I'll love you forever."

"Let me carry you over the threshold, Terry Lynn. I know it's a little old-fashioned, but I like traditions," he said.

Terry Lynn gave Willie a passionate look, and sighed, and said, "Willie, I would love for you to carry me over the threshold."

So he picked her up into his arms and spun around and carried her through the doorway, into their home. They looked at *each* other, kissed, and when he gently released Terry Lynn from his arms onto the floor, they hugged for a few sentimental moments.

"You're so beautiful, Terry Lynn."

"I'm happier than I've ever been in my entire life Willie."

"Yeah, Terry Lynn, I'm completely satisfied now. Life couldn't be any better than it is right now."

Then he held her tightly and kissed her again.

"This is wonderful Willie and I'm so glad that we already have our home. It was here just waiting for us."

"Yeah, Terry Lynn, our home wasn't the only one waiting for us to come back to," said Willie with raised eyebrows and clinched lips, along with a little smirk on his face.

"Oh boy, Willie, we're going to be in so much trouble with our families once they get hold of us. We didn't tell them a thing about what we did while we were away."

"Well, we didn't plan to get married while we were away," said Willie. "It *just felt right in our hearts* to go ahead and do it. Besides you have a great idea about having a second ceremony."

"We can have one of the biggest weddings in the county!" exclaimed Terry Lynn.

"Now, remember, if you want a huge wedding, we'll have to tuck away a little more money. One day we'll be ready to have the kind of wedding that we really want to have."

"You can say that again. Our families would be furious with us if we didn't have a ceremony for them to come to," said Terry Lynn.

Then those two decided that they didn't want to call, to let anyone know that they were back home quite yet. Instead, they wanted to spend more time alone together, to enjoy their moments back home together as a newly married couple.

After a couple of hours passed, they decided that they were ready to call Willie's brother, Charles. Willie wanted Charles to be the first one to hear the great news.

Charles answered the phone and Willie was so excited about his news that it was the first thing he said to Charles. He thought it was the best way to start the conversation.

"Charles, you're now talkin' to a married man!"

"Are you kiddin' me, Willie? That's real nice, but hold on for a minute now—What happened to our wedding invite? You know what? I don't believe anyone else told me that they received an invitation either. What's goin' on little brother? Just wait. I'm coming over there. Don't go anywhere. I'll see you in a few minutes."

So Charles went to their home and as soon as Willie answered the door, Charles said, "Now, what's goin' on?"

"Hey slow down and stop worrying 'cause we didn't have a fancy wedding. It just happened. Charles, I just looked at her big green eyes, lookin' up at me. Everything felt so right. I just knew then, that I had to have her for the rest of my life. She joked a little bit about my proposal. She said she guess she better say yes right then, 'cause I might not have the courage to ask her again for a few years. We drove to the justice of the peace that same night."

"Why? You know we've talked about having a big shin dig 'n' everything. You know, a country band, dancin' and all that good stuff. Look now, Willie . . . it's a near miracle that you finally found the girl of your dreams. We started to give up on you years ago. We figured if it didn't happen when you were in your twenties, it wasn't going to happen at all."

"Very funny," said Willie. Then he said, "I just needed to find the right woman. I had to be sure and now I am sure. There isn't a woman on earth that's more right for me than Terry Lynn. Listen now, just because I wasn't in a rush like the rest of y'all, doesn't mean it wasn't ever going to happen. Terry Lynn and I are truly in love, and we always will be. We just couldn't wait any longer, you know-the mood was right and the time was right to go ahead and make it happen. Besides, Terry Lynn and I discussed all of those other issues and we decided to have a huge ceremony a little later."

"Well, I guess so, but I want to know how long, is a little later? I know you two are a little strapped for cash right now. I mean I know you're managing your expenses, but you sure don't have enough for a big wedding. I know what I'm going to do. I'm going to get together with mama, and daddy, and the rest of the family, about giving y'all the kind of wedding the two of you deserve to have. We're all going to chip in so you and Terry Lynn can have your dream wedding soon. You know that mama and daddy want to do this. They've been waiting for this to happen for a long, long time. This will be a wedding that our town can really talk about. Ooooh boy! We're goin' to have some fun!!"

"Hey Charles, are you still goin' to be my best man, like we talked about in the past?" asked Willie.

"Well, hell yeah! You bet I am."

Terry Lynn ran over to Charles and gave him a big hug and thanked him.

"I hope Rae Ann finds the right man for herself someday. She deserves to have a man that she can call her own. I think Heather and Trish would like that too. Now, I need to call her. She's probably wondering where in the world I've been."

"You bet she has been. I know she's been pretty upset with you Willie boy. The last time I spoke with her, she told me that she's planning to have a talk with you, and with you too, Terry Lynn."

"Uh oh," replied Terry Lynn.

"Don't worry right now 'cause I don't think y'all are going to have that talk today and I'll tell you why. I was out for a while earlier today, and when I got back home, there were some messages on my answering machine." Then Charles hesitated because he was reluctant to tell Willie anything that could upset him, since he and Terry Lynn just got home.

"Willie, when you first called, I thought there was a chance that Rae Ann had been with you and Terry Lynn. Of course, now that I know what the two of you were up to, I'm starting to worry and I'm afraid that Aaron, Heather, and Trish might be right. They're afraid that Rae Ann is missing and they've gone searching for her."

Charles, now started to feel concern, since no one heard from Rae Ann for a little over a week. Rae Ann spoke with her daughters before she took off, and told them that she had some personal matters to take care of. She said for them not to worry, 'cause she was going to take some time to relax, and maybe visit some old friends. Since their mother sometimes took time to spend alone, out of town, they didn't worry, up until now. She's never been away for this long.

CHAPTER 18

Heather and Trisha knew something had to be wrong. Heather wanted to speak to Aaron about her sister's and her own suspicions, so she decided that she should do it right away. He could help them decide exactly how they were going to handle this situation.

"Aaron honey, uh . . . I know you believe that I worry too much about things sometimes; especially, if it concerns our mama, but I feel it in my gut this time. I think something is terribly wrong and Trish thinks so too."

"Well Heather, I wish I could tell you that you're making too much of this, but your mama hasn't been in touch with any of us for over a week now. She hasn't called anyone as far as we know. She really shouldn't handle things this way."

"Aaron, what do you mean—*handle things*? What things and in what way? What are you talking about?"

Aaron's face was flushed and it looked a little distorted as he closed his eyes and crinkled his nose while rubbing his hand against his cheek, as he contemplated on what he was going to tell Heather. He could feel the hard stare that Heather gave him. All he could think of to do was to look away.

"Aaron, what kind of a look is that? Aaron, look at me. I've never seen that kind of look on your face before. Aaron, are you okay? Oh, now wait a minute. I know why I've never seen that look on your face before. It's because you never hid anything from me before have you? Not until now anyway. You and mama have a secret don't y'all? What is it Aaron? What are you hiding from me? Please, I'm really worried, so you need to tell me."

"Now, Heather, you know about doctor and patient confidentiality.'

"You can't use that reason Aaron. You're not mama's doctor anymore. Why did you stop being her doctor anyway? No, wait! Just save it until Trish gets here! I'm sure my sister wants to hear what you have to say."

"I was her doctor when she swore me to secrecy, so I'm still bound by law and by ethics. She never consented to let you girls know about her health. It was something that she wanted to do herself."

"Her health? Aaron, what's the matter with my mama? I need to know right now."

"Well, honestly, I'm not sure what's going on with your mother right now. She could have decided to stay longer. Maybe, taking care of things, is taking longer than she expected. She wanted her privacy, so she could think about some things."

"Think about what things Aaron?"

"You'll have to ask her that when you talk to her. That's all I can say for now."

"This is just so unusual for mama to behave this way."

"Well, she told y'all that she was going away. She is an adult."

Then there was a knock at the door. It was Trish.

"Thank goodness you're here now, Trish," Heather said with a sigh of relief.

Trish noticed the tension between Heather and Aaron. "What in the world is going on between the two of you? Heather, I don't think you've ever been angry with Aaron."

"No, I have never ever been upset with Aaron before, but there's a good reason for it now. Tell her Aaron," said Heather with a stone cold look on her face.

"Tell her what Heather? I'm just not sure that we truly have anything to worry about."

"No offense Aaron," said Trish, "but I believe that my sister has a genuine concern 'cause our mama has never been away from us for this long."

"Well, maybe she did try to reach y'all. Have you checked all of your messages from the past day or two? Do you think that she might have let someone else know because she couldn't reach either one of you? Maybe she talked to Willie. We don't even know where he's been. He has a way to just up 'n' leave, too."

Heather looked at him in dismay and said "Aaron, I don't think you even believe what you're saying. Are you really convinced that there's a logical reason for her to not even call us by now, to let us know that she's going to be away longer than she thought? She used to tell Heather and me if she was going to be gone for a few hours. This just doesn't make any sense."

Aaron looked at her and thought about what she just said. What if Rae Ann is up to something? What if she isn't planning to be around? He knew that if Rae Ann wasn't planning to be around, it wasn't in the way that Heather and Trish thought. Now, he was afraid that she might be planning her own death. He didn't want to tell Heather or Trish what he suspected. He needed to be sure first. Aaron looked at Trish and looked at his wife again, and said "You're right Heather. I'm not convinced that everything is all right. I know that she would have found some way to contact someone first. Things just don't add up. She wouldn't have left us clueless like this unless something is seriously wrong."

"Hmm, it's like you just said, Aaron," said Trish . . . "Well, have y'all got any ideas?"

"Yeah," said Aaron, and then he continued to say . . . We need to go to her house and search for any clues that might be there. Maybe there's a note there. We can check her phone messages and the phone numbers on her caller ID to help us find her."

Heather fondly looked at Aaron and nodded and said, "Now you're talking, honey. That's a great idea. Let's get going."

Aaron, Heather, and Trish rushed out the door, and when they arrived at the house, they looked through their mama's papers without any hesitation. They listened to the phone messages and read her appointment book. They found a paper with their favorite restaurant written on it, and dated the day their mama disappeared.

Trish said that she would call the restaurant to find out if a reservation had been made. They also checked for any clue that they could find—any messages, receipts but didn't find anything that could be helpful. Aaron then found a diary and said, "Hey girls, we might have something now." He didn't mention that he was sure he knew some of the secrets written in their mother's diary. He decided to let them find out for themselves.

Trish then said, "I didn't even know that mama kept a diary."

Then Heather said, "That makes two of us."

"Well sis, what does it say?" asked Trish.

Heather answered, "I'm going to start reading from three weeks ago until present."

"Okay," said Trish. "Maybe now, we can finally find something out."

"Trish, mama has been keeping secrets. Oh no, this isn't good at all. I can't believe she didn't tell us anything at all about this."

"Dern it, Heather! Can you please read it out loud? What does it say?"

"Mama's sick. She's real sick. The doctors believe that she has something called **Polyarteritis Nodosa** and sometimes it's fatal. She wrote that she isn't sure if she was going to have the treatments for it and she wasn't ready to tell us yet."

Trish felt like she needed to sit down. "How could she keep this from us? Well, I know where her files are and where she keeps her mail. I'm going to see if I can find copies of her medical records or maybe I'll find her bills. We need to learn all we can about it and about how she's feelin' right now." Then she got up and walked down the hall to the study.

Aaron was already in there. Trish said, "Aaron, we know mama's ill. Heather read it in mama's diary, so if you already have copies of her medical records, I would like to see them now, please."

Aaron looked at the documents that he had taken out of the file cabinet before Trisha entered the room. Then Aaron said, "Okay, there's nothing confidential about this now. There are some documents here. You girls might want to read them, but I'm going to leave the room before you two do. Let it not be said that I didn't keep my promise to your mother." Then he walked out of the room.

Trisha then called out to Heather and said, "Hey sis, you better come in here. I'm in mama's study. I think we need to read these copies of mama's medical records."

Heather came in and sat down beside her. Trisha decided to read the documents, but for the sake of saving some time, she read only what they needed to know.

"Well, Heather, this document says that mama does have a disease called **Polyarteritis Nodosa**; just as you read in her diary. This paper is one of the first documents and look at the date on it. Mama knew about her illness even before the car accident. So that's why she was so secretive. That's why the doctors kept talking to each other but not to us about mama."

Heather nodded her head because she understood and she said, "And that's why there were so many doctors. Yep, this explains everything."

"I didn't even notice any symptoms. She hid it from us, when she felt any pain. I know that she's been spending less and less time with us. Now, we know why."

Trish went on, to read that it's an idiopathic disease, but they are making progress and although without treatment the chance of survival is poor, with treatment, a person's symptoms will improve and the chance of long-term survival is more likely.

"Trish, what is mama's prognosis? Has mama had any treatments at all? How in the world could she keep all of this from us?"

"Heather, it says that mama has taken prednisone and cyclophosphamide and that she has consented to try some new drug to help prolong her life. She's also donated plasma from time to time to help various medical institutions with hope to learn about the illness and find a cure or an antidote. It also cuts down on the costs of her treatments and helps her earn a little extra spending money from time to time."

"Well, that's good. Do you see the date of her most recent treatment?"

"Well, Heather, it appears that she's missed a few treatments."

"I'm going read her diary again because I think she wrote something in it two or three weeks ago."

She picked the diary up and read about Rae Ann's thoughts and feelings about continuing to live.

"Trish? Aaron? I think mama might want to die. We've got to find her right now."

They were both angered and pained by what their mother had kept from them.

Then Trisha looked at the time and said, "We don't really have much time until it's dark and we still need to try to find out where she is right now. If there's anything else for us to know about her illness, we can ask Aaron."

"Are you sure about that Trish?" asked Heather.

At that moment, Aaron had walked to the entrance of the office and said, "Let me answer that Heather. Yes, you can ask me anything about the disease now and I'll tell you everything that I know. I know you're angry and hurt, but you have to know that I quit being your mama's doctor because I didn't want to deal with the information that I knew and the emotional involvement and have to face you and your family each day, knowing what I did. I've been torn between ethics, confidentiality, and my emotions. It's just so difficult. By discontinuing as her doctor, I'm pretty much in the same shoes as you and Trish, because basically, I'm now limited to the information concerning your mother. We're in this together as a family. I don't want to hide anything from you anymore. I'm so sorry honey. Please forgive me."

Trisha said, "Okay, you two can talk about it a little later and hopefully, when mama is with us, since we've got a thing or two to fuss at her about too. If it was up to me though Heather, I'd be inclined to forgive him. His intentions are good and the poor man's hurtin'. Just look at him."

"Right now, we've got to figure out where she is, Trish."

Aaron then said, "Well, I've already called and they've also confirmed that she hasn't had any more treatments, other than what we've seen on the documents. The specialists at the hospital haven't heard a word from her either. She hasn't scheduled anything. I'll check with the other hospitals and treatment centers to see if she's registered as a patient with any of them."

"Well, all we've got right now is the restaurant to check. I'll call it and see if she went there at any time."

So Trisha called and the restaurant to confirm that their mother had made a reservation for two, about a week earlier.

"All we can do is head out that way. That is her favorite restaurant and the river's nearby and we all know how much she loves it at the river."

"Well, okay then, we'll take our car," Aaron said. Then they fled out the door and drove to the restaurant. If they couldn't find anything else out at the restaurant, they'd go to the river.

"All right, now I think we'll all agree that it's time to call the police," said Heather.

"Yeah, I'm doing that right now," said Aaron. Then Heather just looked into his eyes. His and her eyes filled with tears.

"Heather, I'm sorry, baby."

"You ought to be," she remarked. "I do love you, Aaron. I know that you didn't mean any harm. Your intentions are always good in everything you do and I forgive you, but honey, you better not ever even think about hiding anything from me again."

"You can bet that I won't. I've learned quite a bit from this experience and I love you way too much to ever disappoint you again."

"I do somewhat understand, Aaron. I'm sorry that I was so harsh."

"It's okay honey. I love you."

"I love you too," said Heather and then they kissed.

"All right you two. Things are obviously good between y'all again and I must say that I'm glad, but can y'all just save the mush until we get back home, whenever that is."

They all smiled and nothing else was said in the car. Their hearts ached; hoping that they'd soon find out more information, as to where Rae Ann could be.

At the restaurant, couple of the employees recognized them and one remembered the conversation with Trisha on the phone earlier that day.

Trish said, "Hi there. I believe I spoke to one of you earlier about our mother. Is there anything more that you can tell?"

One of the two employees said, "Well, all I can really tell you is that she didn't look like she felt very well. She looked kinda pale and she coughed a lot. Like I told you when we spoke, she called about two weeks ago, and made a reservation for two, and was here nine days ago, and she was alone. She ate, she left, and she hasn't been in here since. Oh, but you know what? I do recall her saying something about going to the river. That's all I know. We certainly wish y'all the very best of luck, and if we see or hear anything else about her, we'll be sure to contact you."

Trish thought for a moment and then said, "You have our home phone numbers, but we'll give you our cell phone numbers, too."

"Okay then ladies, it looks like we're making some progress," commented Aaron.

"Yeah, let's get going now—as quick as we can," said Heather. "I think we'll find her."

Trish also felt they were on the right track, as they headed for the river.

About half way there, Aaron called the police and the medical specialists again, to let them know exactly where they were headed. He had his medical bag with him and was prepared to help Rae Ann in giving her necessary medical attention until they could get her to the hospital. They left the message on Charles's answering machine and briefly told a few others about the situation.

Back at Willie and Terry Lynn's house, Willie was angry and astounded by the news Charles gave him about Rae Ann. His reaction came as no surprise to Charles or to Terry Lynn.

"What? What are you tellin' me? I'm goin' to get my rifle right now!" said Willie

"Willie, don't do anything without givin' it a lot of thought. You're too angry right now and too emotional. It's scaring me. I don't want anything to happen to you," Terry Lynn said with tears in her eyes. She was starting to feel some nervous anxiety over the thought of Willie involving any kind of weapon in this situation.

Charles said, "Willie, she's right. Maybe we better wait until we hear from them first, and then you and I can head on out and meet up with them or even look for her on our own."

"All right Charles; I'll give them one hour to call. If they don't call us in an hour, or if I don't hear from you then, I'm going to go find them. You hear me? I'll be damned if I sit here all day—doin' nothing," Willie said as he shook his fist while he held the rifle up high, pointing the barrel upward, but with his finger on the trigger.

Then Charles said, "Hey be careful with that Willie. You haven't used that rifle in years. Maybe you should put it down."

"It ain't loaded yet," said Willie. "It'll be loaded before I leave here though. I need it just in case there's a reason to use it. I bet Randy's back in town, after all this time."

Terry Lynn burst into tears and said, "Willie, honey, don't worry. Everything is going to be all right." Then she threw her arms around him.

"Okay, I better get goin' now. You call me if you need me to come back over here, Willie. On second thought, maybe I should stay here for a while longer."

"No, you go on home, Charles."

Charles said, "Terry Lynn, don't you worry about a thing, either. We can guarantee that we'll find all of them, and your new husband will be back home with you before you know it. The news just kinda *threw him for a loop,* and it got me right upset, too, so we need to take care of this. Well anyway, I better get goin' now. Talk to y'all in a bit. Bye now."

"Bye."

"I don't believe this, Terry Lynn. I'm tellin' ya that something's really stinkin' about this whole situation. I still think it's the one that we've always called the *Dirt Man*. I think he's behind all of this. I think we all know him too and I still think Randy's got something to do with it. I can't believe that anyone has gotten away with this all these years. A lot of our folks have gone through a living hell every day of their lives, not knowing where their family members are or if they're even living anymore. This just can't go on for much longer. Why would anyone want to destroy people's lives like that?"

"Willie, he's the worst kind of criminal. He's a psycho who's really sick in the head. But you should just calm down and try to relax until we hear from Charles. You shouldn't go out lookin' by yourself. Whether you stay here or go out searchin' for them, you'll still need your strength. You'll feel better if you eat anyway."

"No, I can't. Enough time's been wasted already."

"I know. I just don't want to let you go. I'm scared, Willie. Why do you have to be the one to go?"

"You need to get used to it. Remember what we talked about, and the decision that I made about my future?"

"Yes, I sure do, and I understand. Now, listen to me. Please, don't you dare get hurt."

"I'll be real careful, Terry Lynn, and I'll come home just as soon as I can. I love ya."

"I love you, too, honey. I insist that you take something to eat with you. It'll only take a couple of minutes for me to make a sandwich."

"Okay, that sounds good."

Then Terry Lynn went to the kitchen. "Willie? Are you sure you don't want to wait for Charles?"

"Yeah, 'cause an hour's too long. You need to call and tell him that I couldn't wait."

Terry Lynn didn't like Willie's decision to not wait, so she prolonged the time. She hoped if she stretched out the time, the phone might ring, but there was still no call from Charles or anyone else. Willie grew impatient and stood up, and headed towards the door.

"Terry Lynn, I'm goin' and I mean, right now."

"No, you should wait Willie. At least call your brother and talk to him about it."

"Charles would have called me if there was any news at all, so there's no need for me to call him. I wondered why it was takin' you so long to make that sandwich."

"I'm going too."

Willie snapped at her and said, "Oh no, you're not! I don't know what's going to happen to you out there and you need to stay here in case they do finally call with any news. I need to make sure that you'll be safe too, so make sure you keep all the doors and the windows locked. There's a pistol locked up in the drawer in the bedroom, too. Here, Terry Lynn. Take this key to unlock the drawer. You know how to use that pistol. Do you want to call someone to come here and stay with you?"

"No Willie. I'll be fine. You call me!"

"I'll try, but it probably won't be until I find something out."

Then he kissed her and walked out the door.

CHAPTER 19

Terry Lynn was thinking that if Willie thought for one little minute that she was going to stay there alone without him while he was out there all alone, he better think again because she wasn't about to stay at home.

They owned two cars and a pickup truck, so after Willie drove away in his car, Terry Lynn got into the other car and drove away. She followed Willie. She kept her distance between them, so he wouldn't know that she was in the car behind his. She knew it would be difficult to stay out of his sight, but it wouldn't be impossible.

She followed Willie down a road that they hadn't been on in years. It was one of the roads that were still off limits to the children in the neighborhood. No child dared to go alone on the forbidden paths in those woods even now. That wooded area still held too much sadness and horrific memories. This was starting to feel a little scary. The next thing she knew, he stopped the car near a ditch and he got out and just stood beside his car. Then he reached downward into his car. Then he took something out. Terry Lynn saw that he was holding a camera. She thought carrying a camera was a good idea although she didn't have a camera with her. What did he see? Then she saw him take pictures of the ditch. The ditch was huge! Now she understood. She didn't remember that ditch being there before; especially a ditch that large. Right now, she felt like she was having too much fun spying on her new husband, but she knew that if he found out that she was there, he'd make sure that she'd turn around and go back home. She didn't dare shout out to him. Just then, she heard a strange noise and turned her head around. She exclaimed, "What is that damn noise back there?" When she turned her head back around, Willie and his car were clear out of sight.

Maybe he saw someone or something, and wanted to take more pictures. She hoped that he hadn't gone too far away. She wondered how he could just disappear so quickly. She became worried and decided to do something about it—but what was she was going to do? She picked up her cell phone and held it, still contemplating her next move. She turned her radio on and sat, trying to stay calm. She felt foolish; wondering how she could possibly come up with a plan. Willie always took charge of things. A few minutes later, Terry Lynn had no time left to make a plan because the glass on the driver's side of her car was suddenly shattered by someone's fist and she was hit by the enormous fist in her nose. The car door was then unlocked and opened, and she was dragged out of the car. Just as she started to open her eyes, that same fist was thrust right back into her face and she became unconscious.

When she regained consciousness, Terry Lynn's eyes were covered, her wrists were bound and tied up together with a piece of rope and her mouth was gagged with a dirty, smelly rag. She couldn't see anything.

She was dragged through dirt and mud, through filthy, grimy areas, with her blood strewing down her from her face, over her clothes. She was dragged by her hair and lifted up and thrown into a vehicle. Sometime later, the vehicle stopped moving and someone was thrown into the vehicle on top of her. The pain was excruciating. She almost wished that she was still unconscious. Terry Lynn groaned with misery, and she was helpless just as the one that was tossed on top of her was. She felt something else touching her, but she couldn't tell if it was someone who'd already been there.

About an hour later, they stopped again, and they were both tossed into another vehicle. Terry Lynn thought it might be some sort of truck. It had a repugnant odor. Suddenly they stopped again. Terry Lynn could hear a police radio. Would she be rescued from this insane mess now? If she had only listened to Willie, she wouldn't be in this situation. She should have stayed home.

She could hear a man's voice and then another man's voice. She could hear movement at the rear of the truck where she was. She had been gagged so tight that she couldn't make a sound. Nothing happened. She wasn't rescued from this grave situation. She heard a man say, "Okay, that's fine sir, you can go now. Have a good day."

She was livid about this. How could this be? Was it really a police officer? She wanted to scream and cry. She was sure she was going to lose her life. She trembled and the person with her was also trembling. This was incomprehensible. What were they going to do?

The ride after that was long and bumpy before they stopped again. This time Terry Lynn wasn't put inside another vehicle. She was left on the ground and something thick was tied around her. It felt like a thick, scratchy rope. Then she heard a horse and it sounded like a buggy or a trailer or something similar. Then she could hear a very faint sound nearby. It must have been the other person. Terry Lynn wondered if the other one was tied with a rope just as she had been tied.

The horrible footsteps first sounded close by and then they sounded just a tad distant. Then she could feel herself slowly moving. She was being pulled somehow; faster and faster. It hurts so much!! Then Terry Lynn was unconscious again.

When she opened her eyes again, she was tied to a tree. Ropes were tied around her waist and the tree trunk. This time she could see, although it was mostly a blur. She felt that this might be the last place that she'd ever see.

Her heart ached for Willie. She hoped he went back home. If he did go back home, he's probably realized by now that something was wrong. Terry Lynn ordinarily let Willie know where she was-with the exception of this time, that is. Now, it's the very first time Terry Lynn ever sneaked around behind Willie's back, and now she's become the victim of an insane criminal.

That grotesque murderer better not have gotten his hands on Willie. What's going to happen next? Terry Lynn wondered if she would ever see her new husband again. There was something that she knew and loved about her Willie, and that was how much he enjoyed outwitting crooks. She wasn't sure if anything gave Willie more pleasure (except being married to her, of course), than trying to catch crooks. She thought he should be a policeman or a sheriff, but Willie was content to just help them when they allowed him to. He said a person couldn't be dumber than to want to be a criminal. There was one criminal that everyone knew he had in the back of his mind and that was the *Dirt Man*. Willie said someday, his cousin Rae Ann and him would catch him in his heinous, dirty criminal acts.

Terry Lynn didn't know who the other victim with her was or if there might be more than one. She didn't hear any other voices or groans or cries. She wondered what was going to happen to them. She wondered what led up to their abductions.

Rae Ann didn't know what was about to happen to her either. Very soon, she would find out. She would also end up side by side with another innocent person. There may have been others.

Right now, all she could do was just continue to lie there with the cold, icy water sloshing against her body and over her face, pulling her deeper into the river. She still had no idea of how long she'd been there, and there was still no recollection of what happened to her during the past days or weeks. Now, the song that had been echoing in her mind; repeatedly, as she lay there, while feeling useless, started to make sense. She felt that it could be a message for her, a sign that these could be her final days and at that moment, she thought that this song was significant, so she just sang the song out loud. This song with the simple words that were expressing her emotions and describing her predicament held an abundance of meaning for her. This song could be her saving grace. If she sang it loudly, maybe help would finally come. But then again, it could mean disaster. She decided to take a chance and she started singing as loud as she could because she knew that even though she couldn't walk or run anywhere, she could use her voice as an instrumental tool. Then Rae Ann started singing the song that she'd been hearing in her mind:

> *Floatin', goin' . . .*
>
> *Floatin' on down the river.*
>
> *Downstream, upstream . . .*
>
> *The water sure makes me quiver.*
>
> *Leavin', goin' . . .*
>
> *I might go on forever.*
>
> *See me, hear me . . .*
>
> *The ferocious waves are tryin' to pierce my soul,*
>
> *As I'm tossed against these rocks.*
>
> *The timeless river's got a hold on me,*
>
> *But in the end—I decide what will be.*

This ol' endless river's going to set me free.

See me, hear me—know that . . .

One day—and then she stopped singing because suddenly, before she could sing another verse, she heard some noise-some very disturbing sounds coming from the surrounding wooded area by the riverside. She listened. The sounds weren't of some caring persons or people asking if she was all right or telling her that they'd call for help. She wasn't quite sure now if she should call out, or just start singing again and act as if she hadn't heard anything around her at all. Maybe it was just some animals, but if so, she'd never heard any animal make those horrid sounds. Rae Ann was starting to feel very insecure and frightened. She sensed that something was very wrong. This uneasy feeling she had didn't pass.

Then, out of nowhere, something had lunged out of the woods and ran right for her and was beside her within seconds. Then *thump*! Before she could really see anyone or anything, she felt another horrible, stinging, searing pain and the trickling water and her blouse turned into a red blur. She started to lose the little bit of sight that she had left. She could feel blood streaming down her face. It all happened so quickly. She couldn't turn her head to see if an animal had sprung out of the woods and leaped at her; causing this agony that she was in or if something else had her in its . . . Maybe it was a rock. She just didn't know and she just couldn't move. Everything started to fade away. It was as if she was seeing a mirage swirling all about her. She started feeling weaker and knew that she couldn't keep her eyes open much longer without a struggle. Just as her eyes were going to completely close, she was grabbed and pulled by the roots of her hair. She was too weak and too afraid to scream or yell. She still couldn't tell what or who it was. She was then dragged across the water, the mud, and the dirt, and then there was an abrupt stop, and she was lifted and tossed into something as if she was a piece of meat. She couldn't run. She couldn't do anything. She was so helpless. When she was tossed, she bumped into something and heard a groan. She knew then that there was someone else there. She also knew that it wasn't any animal that bit her. The one that grabbed her and hurt her was a despicable excuse for a human being. All she could do right now, was lay there, partially lying on top of another person. All of a sudden, she was pulled up—by her throat in an upright position, and something was wrapped around her head, and her eyes were then covered completely. Her hands and feet were also tied up. She had been tied up so tightly, that she knew she was bleeding from it. She could feel little tinges of pain from it cutting into her skin. She wondered how long this other person had been there. Undoubtedly, the other person had been harmed too, and Rae Ann wondered how long it would be before they'd both die. She wondered how long ago this other person had been kidnapped.

Rae Ann was in so much pain, and she still felt so weak, but she had to try to stay strong and awake. She needed to listen to voices, to recognize sounds, and to try to get away somehow. She was going to try to help the other person too, if there was any way that she could. Rae Ann thought to herself—this smell is so stagnant and it's making me sick. I want to scream, but I can't. What am I going to do? She then heard a familiar sound. It sounded like a door was closing. Most likely, it was a car door. Now, I hear a motor. We're definitely in a vehicle of some sort. I still think it's a car. I don't hear anyone talking yet. Then the vehicle started moving. She didn't know what direction they were driving. She had no clue as to where they were going. Again, Rae Ann struggled to keep her eyes open for as long as she possibly could, but in a matter of minutes, she was unconscious.

Unsure of how much more time had passed by, Rae Ann awoke again. The car door opened, and she was pulled out of the car by her feet this time. She was too numb and too afraid to try to kick. Then she dropped to the ground and was rolled up in something that felt like burlap or canvas. She could hardly breathe. She didn't know where the other person was. She just couldn't hear any sounds coming from the car. Then Rae Ann was dragged again and picked up and tossed into something else again. She did hear the clanging sound of some sort of metal. Then she felt something beneath her and heard a loud groan at the same moment that Rae Ann groaned from the anguish and the pain that she was in. Rae Ann wanted to speak to the other person, but she was still bound and gagged. She couldn't move her lips and she could barely breathe. She hoped that she could get the gag off her mouth somehow and off her eyes to see the other person and try to talk and make a plan. Rae Ann wanted to tell the other one that she thought that they were now in the back of a pickup truck. She could never forget the lingering foul smell. The truck began moving, and off they went to an unknown destination. Rae Ann's eyes closed once more.

There was another stop. Rae Ann knew it wasn't planned because she heard a police radio, but the police didn't see Rae Ann or the other person, or, people, because the police let the bastard go. After a while they came to another stop and at least one other person was pulled to the ground. Rae Ann was yanked with a great deal of force and dropped to the ground too. She was tied up with a rope and more materials. Then she thought she heard a horse and all of a sudden, she was twisting and turning on the ground. With the rope attached, she must have been pulled for miles. She could feel the prickly road, scraping most of her body as most of her clothing became absorbed with her blood. She knew the person beside her felt every bit of the pain that she felt—that is if the other one was still alive. Was there going to be an end to this cruelty? No, probably not until they were dead.

There was one last stop and the one person that Rae Ann was aware of, was taken and a few minutes later, Rae Ann was cut loose and lifted up and taken too. She passed out once again and when she awoke this time, she was no longer blindfolded. She opened her eyes as much as possible, and tried to look around her without being noticed, but it was no use, because her vision was still poor. She could see very little and it was too difficult to recognize where she was. She wasn't sure if she would know where she was anyway.

When she was tossed to the ground once again, she found that she was in a dismal, rundown, old shed. Some of the wood that it was built with was rotted and all she could see was some sort of basin and a cup on the wooden floor. It was cold, damp, and smelly. There were no windows so she couldn't climb out and she still didn't know for sure if it was day or night. There was some sort of board, a very large board that partially divided the room. Old, rusted garden tools hung on the wall of the shed, along with phone cords, phone lines, pieces of rope, burlap bags, and cloth—like the one that was used to blindfold her with on the way here. Something else very disturbing and trifling was when Rae Ann noticed that a long, tattered, white dress hung on one of the nails on the shed's wall. It looked like a wedding dress. That dress had a stagnant smell just like everything else did. There was also a broken full-length mirror. If there's any truth to the superstition that a broken mirror gives a person seven years of bad luck, it was a fact that it happened to the poor woman who wore that dress. Rae Ann wanted to get a closer look, but she was too afraid to move. For some unknown reason, that dress looked very familiar, but she had no recollection of it right now. Why on earth would anyone hang a dress in a shed? Her hands were still tied up, but they were tied in front of her and her mouth was still gagged so she still couldn't scream. Her clothes were ripped and bloody. Her face, her arms, and her legs were swollen. There was nothing that Rae Ann could do to help herself or anyone else right now, so she just hoped that the morbid, demented creep would just stay away from her for the rest of the day. She then fell over to her side and just curled up as much as she could, burying her head in her arms to form some sort of cushion. If she could possibly sleep for a little while, she might feel a little stronger emotionally and physically, just as she did at the river, and she could exercise her mind to figure a way to escape. Her memories and her music helped her survive before, so that's what she'd do again. She knew deep in her heart that if she was going to die, she wanted to die thinking back to her happiest times. Then she fell asleep.

She managed to sleep for a few hours, but the time swiftly passed by, with the hours feeling like minutes. When she woke up, she saw that there was dry cereal in the cup and a bottle of soda. That meant that someone had been in there while she slept. "Ugh," she muttered as she shrugged her shoulders at that thought. She then had to figure out how she was going to eat and drink with her hands still tied. She really didn't want any of it, but she was so hungry. Her mouth was still gagged with a filthy cloth. How was she supposed to remove it? Maybe it was a sickly little game that the bastard was playing. Maybe he thought about how hungry she was, but didn't want her to eat yet, or maybe he's coming back. The thought of him coming back frightened her. Rae Ann assumed it's a male, because of the strength it took to lift her, but it very well could be a woman.

About half an hour later, she heard footsteps. They sounded like the same heavy footsteps that tormented her cousin Willie and the others in the past. Figuratively, those situations were enough to traumatize any child or adult for the rest of their lives, but Rae Ann was still determined to use her memories to her advantage. She still felt that strength and planning was what it was all about.

Oh no, the door began to open. This would be the first time that she'd see her abductor. Why was she permitted to see him now? She was no longer wearing the blindfold, so she'd be able to identify him. Rae Ann believed, without a doubt, that he intended to kill her. That must be why he doesn't care if she sees what he looks like. She started to shake as the door opened, but then it closed abruptly. What can this mean? At that moment, Rae Ann was relieved that she was still alone and alive. She felt that she was still living by pure grace and that there was a reason for it. She believed it was time for him to suffer the consequences for his actions and she wanted to be the one to make him pay for all the evil he committed. She didn't know if he was the *Dirt Man* or not, but she knew she'd soon find out.

She was afraid to lie back down, so she just sat, staring at the door, hoping that no one would come in. She had thoughts of leaping out at him, just as he leaped out towards her at the river. Little by little, she started to regain feeling in her legs, but she didn't feel that she was strong enough quite yet. Besides, she needed to make a good plan that she was certain would work.

More time passed by, and her back began to ache from sitting, so she just toppled over once again. Her ribs stung with even more pain from sleeping on her side the previous night on the hard, cold floor, so now she positioned herself laterally in the opposite direction. Now, she wasn't facing the door. Rae Ann whispering to herself, "Oh what does it matter? If he comes in, I can't do anything about it anyway. Maybe I'll feel less afraid if I can't see him. Maybe if he realizes that I still don't know what he looks like, he won't kill me—at least not right away." She tried to make up a new song in her mind to prevent some of the insecurity that she felt, but after positioning herself, she soon fell asleep.

Rae Ann woke up to the sound of a gruff voice. She could see someone walking out of the shed. She made sure she was silent, so he wouldn't know that she was watching him. She could see that he was standing at about six feet tall and his hair color is medium brown. When he started to turn towards her, she closed her eyes. He just walked past her and glanced back at her and he walked out the door. Rae Ann thought to herself, "That sure was a close call. Who the hell was he talkin' to and what the hell was he saying? I don't plan to stay in this damn place much longer." She was still bewildered because she didn't know why she was there.

Now he'd taken the cloth out of her mouth. Her gums were bleeding. Now, she saw a small beam of light shining through a crack in the wall. She wanted to get closer to it, but she was still leery about moving away from where she was sitting. She knew that she was going to sneak to take a peek at it soon though.

She noticed a plate of food was on the floor. There was also a spoon. Oh no! There was also a rose which was placed in a tall glass. She was even more confused than before and she felt nothing but disgust. This weirdo must be some kind of pervert. She burst into tears. Her eyes were sore and they hurt even more when she cried, but she cried anyway.

She noticed that the dress was still hanging on the wall, and hoped and prayed that it had absolutely nothing to do with his plans for her.

Rae Ann then tried not to think about how bad of a situation she was in and decided to eat. She needed her strength to get away from there.

While she ate, she noticed that for a brief moment, the beam of light had disappeared. She wasn't sure if someone was outside or if the sun was going down. She just kept eating. She ate as much as she felt she could keep in her system. She pretended that she was eating chicken. That way, she wouldn't have any problem making it stay down. She also ate the dry cereal although it was stale.

She felt a little stronger and she regained some feeling in her legs and in her feet. She was going to start making plans.

She'd try her best to think of a way to escape.

She asked herself out loud, "What would Cousin Willie do if he was here in this shed all locked up with a madman outside? He was always clever. He can outwit almost anyone. Willie boy would take a look at that hole in that crack in the wall to see if there are any weak places surrounding it because then the boards might easily be removed or split into pieces with the proper tool or a heavy, forceful, hard punch. Then because the hole is so close to the door, I can try to reach the door knob, open the door and run for my life. But what if the door has a lock on it? Maybe I can use one these garden tools to break the latch on the door. Maybe the latch is as rusted as these garden tools are."

Another idea is to take the shovel or the hoe that were hanging on the wall, and hit him as soon as he steps inside. Rae Ann started to feel more confident about each of the plans she worked on. She thought it was good to have more than one plan. If one didn't work, then she'd always have a backup plan. She shook and cringed to think about the possibility of being murdered before she would even get the chance to use one of them to save herself. As her mind raced—trying to put each individual part of the plan together, she tried to think of a way to get the tools and other items down from the shed's wall without her abductor noticing that they were gone. She also decided that she'd count on her good instinct as to when she'd put her plan into effect. It was so much easier for her to write it all on paper. She wished that she could do that now.

Now, she needed to go to the bathroom. What was she to do now? She slid herself to the area where the board dividing the room was, and there was an outdoor, portable potty behind that room divider. She had to try to stand up somehow. When she decided to lean against the board, it wobbled. The wobbly, creaking old board with nails extending from it could also be part of a plan.

She still wondered if anyone was searching for her. Where are they now? What are they doing? More of her memory was coming back now. She could remember leaving her house and more specific details. She remembered driving her car recently, but she still wasn't quite sure where she was going. She also remembered that she hadn't told her family goodbye. She already remembered being ill, but she still doesn't remember what sort of illness it is, or if it's lethal.

She also remembered that she had medical documents. She wondered if they'd gone to her home yet and if they found any copies of her medical information or if Aaron decided to tell them the secret that he was forced to keep for Rae Ann. She remembered every word that was said. She also remembered that she had a note in her pocket although she wasn't sure why she had the note. Even though she couldn't remember everything about the note, she was relieved that more of her memory had returned and that things were starting to come together. Hopefully, she'd remember everything she needed to very soon, and then she'd know why she was at the riverside.

Thankfully, the rest of the day was uneventful. She wondered if there were any other victims there and if they were still alive. She wondered if the one that was with her on the way here, was also alive.

There was a chill in the air that night. It was enough of a chill to make Rae Ann feel cold in the musty, old shed. It was another somewhat restless night for Rae Ann. She had a high fever. She wasn't sure if she'd even wake up the next morning. She wondered if she was going to become part of the big beautiful, blue sky before sunrise, whether she was ready to or not. She had no medicine and she felt as if her life was slowly fading away.

Much to her surprise, when she woke up the next morning, she found that she wasn't alone the entire night, because someone had placed a blanket over her. The tools and most of the other items were still hanging on the shed's walls. The only item that appeared to be missing was the white dress.

CHAPTER 20

While it was probable, that the *Dirt Man* had Terry Lynn in his gruesome, murderous clasps; it was definite, that Randy drove to where Willie was, sneaked up on Willie—just as he had in the past, hit Willie, and knocked him down to the ground, put him inside the car, and drove off. When Willie was conscious again, he was no longer inside the car. Willie did manage to get hold of his rifle though and said some things to Randy that he had wanted to say for a very long time. Poor Willie hadn't yet made a connection between the dirt man and Randy although he was very suspicious of this at times through the years.

"You weren't quick enough for me Randy. See what I've got here? I've got my rifle. You're one slow, stupid son-of-a-gun. You've just turned into a big, useless sack of waste. You've never lived like a decent human being in your life. Well, I know you've ruined some of our lives around here. I'll just bet you're guilty of a lot of things. Pretty soon, I'll have you right where I want you—finally behind bars in a prison.

Hey . . . who's jumpin' the gun now Randy? Do you hear me? I asked you a question! Am I jumpin' the gun now? Naw, it looks like you are. How does it feel?" Willie asked Randy as he nudged and poked at Randy with the barrel of the rifle. "How does it feel to be in the front of the barrel instead of holding the trigger? I ought to blow your head off, but I'm going to turn you in to the police."

"You ain't got nothin' on me, Willie boy! You just think you do! What do you think you can prove? You can't prove anything at all," he bellowed, moving his eyes, looking from side to side, as he tried to find an instant to make a move to regain his control over Willie. All Randy could do right now, was to give Willie an eerie, blank stare with his eyes and then snarl in his disgruntled voice and say, "You can't handle me Willie. Just how long do you think you can keep me here with you? You know I'll get away and there's nothin' that you can do about it! You were a little squirt when you were a young kid, and you're still a little squirt! I could spit and it would knock you down flat on your face." Then he grinned.

"Shut up Randy. I'm a man and that's something that you'll never be. Anyone would look small compared to your fat ass."

Right when Willie finished those words, Randy leaped at Willie and then a fight broke out. Willie's phone flew out of his pocket. Randy tried to grab Willie's rifle, but Willie tossed it into his other hand and positioned it like someone who was getting ready to swing at a baseball, but instead of a baseball, he quickly set his sights on Randy and swung at him. Randy then tried to kick him in an attempt to trip him, but Willie was too sharp and too fast for him. Willie swung his rifle at Randy again and this time, Randy swung back with his fist and punched Willie and he fell to the ground—as the rifle was released from Willie's hand. Then he grabbed at Randy's legs and tripped Randy and when Randy fell to the ground, he kicked him in the face until blood started pouring out of his mouth. Willie got up and picked up his rifle.

Randy said, "You dumb idiot, you knocked my teeth loose and now I'm bleeding."

Then Willie said, "I'll do more than that to you, Randy. You won't bully around decent, church-going people much longer. Your time has come."

Then Randy grabbed Willie's leg and Willie fell back down. Randy and Willie continued to wrestle on the ground until Willie knocked Randy *out cold.* Then Willie got up from the ground and picked up his rifle again and ran, leaving his phone behind; back into the woods. Willie realized that his phone fell out of his pocket and he lost his camera, but he knew he couldn't go back. He figured Randy was looking for him by now. He then checked his rifle, only to find that he was out of bullets and his extra bullets were in his car, locked up in his ammunition case. All he could do was to keep moving and to try to get back to his car before Randy did.

By the time Randy woke from his unconsciousness, Willie was nowhere in sight. Willie packed a hard blow to Randy's face and stomach, so he struggled to get up from the ground. Now, he knew just a little bit about what pain felt like.

Randy decided to go back to his home and check on Rae Ann, who was still tied and gagged in his shed. But then paranoia struck Randy's devious, calculative mind when he recalled what Willie had said about his intentions to call the police. Randy decided to camouflage Willie's car—just as he had done with his own car many times. He knew where he parked Willie's car so he walked in that direction, and once he found it, he drove to where he had parked his own car. Randy glanced back in the direction of Willie's car and saw that the brush and the trees camouflaged Willie's car to his satisfaction. He didn't think anyone would ever suspect that there was a car hidden back there. Then he drove down some back roads in his car to his house.

In the meantime, Willie had decided to go back to his car. He took a look around him and although he was never in this particular area, he thought he had a pretty good idea of his whereabouts. If his spare phone was still in the car, he would call the police. Knowing that he still wanted to try to find Rae Ann and the others on his own, he kept walking to where he thought he last saw the car. Once he got there he noticed a problem. His car wasn't there. He was upset but he wasn't about to give up. He still needed to try to find a phone somewhere. He was still feeling sore and a little woozy from the fight, but in his despair, he didn't hesitate to walk. It was a long, grueling day and he knew that he was in store for more challenges ahead. Willie had great determination to see this through.

So Willie walked, and walked, but there was no one in sight. Finally, he saw a building that he recognized and headed towards it. Then he stumbled over a rock and started slipping. He grabbed a limb hanging from a tree to keep him from falling into a large, somewhat rectangular hole in the ground, but the limb wasn't sturdy enough. It snapped in two, and Willie fell into the hole. All he could do now was try to climb out, but it was a difficult task. His mouth still hurt from the fight with Randy and he was tired. Willie decided to rest and then afterward he'd try again to climb up the sides to get out of there, and find help.

So Willie closed his eyes and when he opened them again, he looked at his watch. This is when he learned that the minutes had turned into hours. He didn't quite understand how he could possibly sleep in that slimy, drab, man-made pit in the ground—in the middle of nowhere; but he knew he needed to try, again, to get out of there. He tried repeatedly to climb the walls as he had before he slept. All he could think of to do now was yell as loud as he could, in hopes that someone would hear him. After calling out six or seven times, he gave up. Willie became disgusted at the thought of being trapped there *without a soul* out there that could hear him.

So while Willie was stuck deep down, far into the ground, about ten or more feet under, Rae Ann was still back inside the shed.

Rae Ann could now hear footsteps and with her eyes focused on the door knob, she saw it turn. She was afraid and tried not to make a sound. She pretended to be asleep. With her head curled up into her folded arms, she tried to peek as this felonious feign walked over to the shed wall. With only one of her eyes barely opened, she saw him hang up that atrocious looking white dress. It was placed back on the hook, on the shed wall. Now it appeared to be somewhat clean. She wondered why someone would even bother to wash it. It was ragged looking and torn and in her opinion, it should have been tossed into the trash.

In a split second, a hand grabbed her throat and then it moved to her head, with his fingers reaching through her tangled, uncombed hair close to the roots. She wanted to scream in pain, but she couldn't make a slight sound. She tried to gasp for air, but she didn't feel like she could even breathe. Then he yanked her off the ground and dragged her outside of the shed, through the grass, to a pond. He untied the filthy cloth and removed it from her mouth. Finally, she could breathe, but only for a quick moment, because her entire body was then submerged underwater. She did manage to hold her breath for as long as she possibly could, but the task was too difficult. After a minute—which felt like an enormous amount of time, she was unable to hold her breath any longer and her mouth filled with water. She started to gag. This was just one of many of his callous acts. Her eyes were opened and she could see him. He just laughed with his cold, morbid, taunting laugh, as he bobbed her head up and down in the pond, watching the bubbles and foam coming from her nostrils and from her mouth. Finally, he pulled her out and told her that he needed to resuscitate her. At that point, she felt she'd rather be dead than for him to put his lips on her. She hoped she'd vomit on him as he tried to touch her face. Instead, he just mumbled a few words to her.

"Rae Ann? How are you feelin' honey? I've got you all cleaned up now. You sure are a strong woman Rae Ann and you're the one for me. I thought Sue might be the one for me a little while back, but she's a weakling. She can't handle a real man like me, but girl—they don't get any stronger than you. I just need to tame you a bit and then you'll make a fine wife for me. I can't let you get dirty now, so I'll carry you to the shed to get your dress, so you can get all prettied up for me." Then he picked her up and carried her in his arms while humming the tune to the *Wedding March.*

Back at the shed, he intended to dress her, but fortunately for her, something or someone distracted him. He looked angry and said, "I'll be back for you." Then he scowled and said, "Now get your dress on Rae Ann. I want you to have yourself fixed up real pretty by the time I get back. Now, **no tricks! Do you hear me?**" Then he left in a hurry.

He thought he knew where Willie would be. He was sure that he would try to find his car, so that's where Randy decided to go. Again, Randy had Willie boy right where he wanted him—in his grave.

She was so relieved that he left. She said aloud, "No tricks? Well, he better just think again 'cause I'm getting out of this hellhole today!"

Rae Ann looked and saw that her hands that were tied together earlier were now free. There were cuts, scratches, and bruises on her wrists and on her arms. Her ankles were no longer bound together either. Hadn't he realized that she could move around freely? She was a little hesitant of walking to the hole in the wall, and looking out of it, or, to check to see if the door was unlocked. She figured that someone else could be involved and they very well might be outside, just waiting for her to attempt to escape, or that he actually had forgotten to tie her back up before he left. Maybe he's playin' another one of his sick games and he's actually out there waitin' for her; testing her, to see what she'll do once she's untied and thinks she's been left alone.

Instead, she knew she was strong enough now to detach the long, wobbly board that was used to divide the room. She was right! She pulled it as hard as she could. It just wouldn't budge, so she grabbed the old, rusty shovel and hacked at the board. Finally, it came loose. She shook it vigorously from side to side until it came up. She gripped the board tightly in her hands, clenching the board with all her might, placing it behind her. She knew that it was a chance that he'd see it if he looked through the hole in the wall, so it stayed behind her the entire time. She waited anxiously for as long as she had to for the moment to fight with him; the moment of revenge.

Suddenly, she heard a vehicle pull up. It sounded like the truck. Rae Ann was nervous and filled with anxiety. The door opened and Randy stepped inside the shed. "Ah girl, I thought I told you to get prettied up for me! Now, don't you give me any problems 'cause I've already got enough of 'em. Nothing is goin' quite right for me today except when I had you in the water. I'm not sure where he scurried off too. The little squirt won't get far though 'cause I know every square inch of these woods out here. It just kinda agitates me when something goes wrong; especially on our wedding day Rae Ann. We have to postpone the wedding for a couple of hours." Then he grunted.

"Yeah Rae Ann, that little fella's goin' to pay the price for him spoiling our special day. I won't kill him just yet. I'll just make him wish that I had killed him right away though. I see you didn't leave me when I took off in the truck. Now, come on over here and give me a kiss before I go back out. We don't have much time Rae Ann. I believe the police have a search party out a few miles away from here."

"Where are you goin' Randy? Are you implying that you have some things to take care of before you marry me?"

"Yeah, I have something that I have to do. The police are getting' a little too close for comfort. I have to put things back on track. Hey, why didn't you put your dress on like I told you to do?"

"I was just waiting here for you Randy. I also have something to take care of. I've planned it just for you. So what do think of that?"

"I don't like surprises much, so before I go back out, you can tell me what it is Rae Ann."

"Oh, I'll do better than that. I'll show you. Just hang tight. I'll show you shortly."

"Oooh wee—Rae Ann! You sure know how to get the heat goin' in here!"

"Where have you been these past years Randy? Have you been here the whole time?"

"Most of the time."

"What about your family? Are they still around too or did they move away? Don't you want them at the wedding?"

Randy became very uncomfortable with Rae Ann's questions. He didn't want her to ask any questions concerning his family, so he answered by saying "It's a surprise Rae Ann. It looks like we both have a surprise for each other. I think you better stop asking so many questions now. It's not something that I find to be appealing for a woman. I need you to come over here to me, **right now**."

Rae Ann didn't want to go near him, but she was afraid that she couldn't stall him any longer. She thought of one more thing to say to him that could help her keep her distance from him. She said, "All right Randy. I won't ask any more questions. I'm sorry. Randy, you know, they say that a fiancé shouldn't see or fondle his new bride in her wedding dress before they're married. I'm just tryin' to stick with tradition, so you're not terribly upset with me are you?"

"I guess not. Just come over here anyway. I want you to stand close to me."

Rae Ann felt nothing but repulsion toward him and she then said, "How about I meet you halfway Randy?"

He started walking towards her and then Rae Ann shouted, "No! No! I can't believe this! You prick! You're despicable! How did you get away with it all these years? A lingering moan and heart wrenching cries were made by Rae Ann. In despair she said, "So, you really are the *Dirt Man*! We just knew that you were involved in these murders somehow. It's all true about you ain't it? As children, we spent countless hours, wondering who the *Dirt Man* was. Was anybody else involved? Answer me! If you want to live a little bit longer, you better tell me where you put the bodies of the ones you killed. Then the anger she felt, built up within her more and more and then she said, "You murderer!" She only uttered the words, "You killed our loved ones. How could you do it to our relatives and to our friends?" Rae Ann then felt so much grief and emotional pain that the tears flowed heavily down her cheeks. Then there was a moment of silence and then she yelled and pointed her finger at him and scornfully said, "You killed so many people. I hate you! You hear me? I hate you! We all hate you! All the rage that had manifested inside her, burned with a vengeance, and she was just about out of control and shouted again to Randy, "Well now Randy, you're not going to make anyone suffer anymore! I'm going to kill you!" Rae Ann was angered at the thought of Randy defying the odds of getting caught by Virginia police long before now. However, she was sure that he'd pay for all the deplorable crimes that he committed through years. She wanted him to pay with his life right now. She said, "I've been waiting for years for this moment. Now, I know for sure, who you are, what you've done, and I can prove it now. Willie and me got you now you son-of-a-bitch! You're goin' to die! There's no need for you to even say a prayer 'cause nothing can or wants to help someone as evil as you are! You're too low-life to even meet your maker. You're going to go straight to hell where you belong."

"Is there anyone else involved in this with you? Is your family part of this too? Are they around here?"

"I can't tell you anything about them and I won't anyway, so you can forget about askin' that question. It'll get you nowhere."

She was angry and said, "Oh we'll find out whether you tell me or not. You better believe it." Now, she had just one more question that she knew he'd better answer.

"Now for your last moments to live, you can tell me where my cousin is. Tell me now! Where is he? I asked you where Willie is. Now answer me!"

"I don't know where he is, Rae Ann. I can tell you that he loves his woman though and that I've got a special place for those two. It was meant for Willie, but after seeing his new wife, I made plenty of room for the both of them. Yeah, they're like you and me Rae Ann. They'll live together and they'll die together."

Rae Ann was so infuriated by what Randy had just said and she wasn't going to let another moment go by. She leaped towards Randy with her leg in the air, and kicked Randy just as hard as she could in the groin. Randy couldn't keep up with Rae Ann's quick action. By the time he realized that she was coming after him, Rae Ann had already grabbed the huge board that she hid so well, with the long, rusted, jagged nails protruding from it and hit him repeatedly over his head, and then she hit his face, his stomach, and everywhere else that she could with every bit of strength that she had. When he dropped down to the floor and looked like he couldn't move anymore, she put the board on top of him, placing one of her hands against the wall in back of her, anchoring one foot at the bottom of the wall too, and placed her other foot against the board, being ever so careful to keep her weak, shaky body from falling to the floor and then she thrust the one foot into the board repeatedly, forcing the long, nails to jab deeper and deeper into Randy's skin. Rae Ann felt no emotion at this point. She just looked at him without expression; going through the motions over and over again until she was too weak to do this any longer, and grabbed a long phone line that was within reach of her; fighting against her weakness and her breathlessness, and wrapped it around his wrists, feet, and his limber neck, tying them as tightly, and as securely, as she could.

"Hey, Randy! You left your tools here. I know you won't hurt anybody anymore, so there now, you stupid, smug bastard. Your only marriage is with death. Yes siree! This was meant to be. What I've done to you today is for every victim and for my grandma, and for my granddaddy, and for all of my relatives. You'll never, ever hurt anybody again! Not ever!"

Then she ran out of the door, and ran until she saw a horse nearby. She realized it was the horse used to drag her to the shed. It was Ol' Nell. She belongs to Randy's family. Rae Ann tried to climb up on Ol' Nell because she thought she'd ride her to go find help. She just couldn't though, because weakness had overcome her once again. Ol' Nell was old and thin. Rae Ann wondered when she was last fed. Ol' Nell didn't appear to have much life left in her either, and Rae Ann decided to set her free, so she could enjoy whatever time she had left. Once she took off the harness and the reins, Ol' Nell trotted across the field. She looked beautiful as her mane flowed in the breeze. Ran Ann hoped that she would be happy now and could live the way that a horse really should live. There was a farm a few miles away where the Colson family lived. They would love to keep Ol' Nell for themselves. Nell would have an abundance of food and water if they kept her. She hoped that they were still living there.

The Colson family felt a lot of resentment towards Randy's family from earlier years because their daughter Lori disappeared like so many others, and like all the other victims of these deadly incidents in the past, they just couldn't prove that Randy's family were the ones responsible for any of the crimes.

Now, Rae Ann knew that there was plenty of proof, but unfortunately, it was probably too late for the Colson family, and for a lot of the others, because Rae Ann was unsure that anyone who was abducted was still alive.

Then, Rae Ann remembered that someone else was in the car with her when she was first taken. Although she was hesitant and still very afraid, she knew that she had to go back and try to find the other person. She then turned around and walked a few feet and saw something or someone tied to a tree. There was a lot of blood so it made it difficult to see what or who it was, but at that point, she was hopeful that it was the other victim, and she was determined to find out if he or she was still alive. As she got closer, she was astonished to see who it was and yelled "Oh my dear heavens! Terry Lynn? Terry Lynn? Is that you?" So the other victim with her was Terry Lynn. Rae Ann waved her arms in the air in an attempt to draw attention. She did draw attention and then she heard her say "Rae Ann, be careful! Don't let the *Dirt Man* see you Rae Ann!"

Once Rae Ann reached the tree where Terry Lynn was, she stopped and she stood as she smiled and said, "Don't worry Terry Lynn. He won't be on our country roads ever again or anywhere else for that matter 'cause I killed him. Can you walk at all? Once, I get you untied, that's what you'll need to do because I don't see anything that I can use to carry you in. You can lean on me if you need to though. If there's no one around here to help us, we'll need to find the truck."

"I don't want to ride in Randy's truck. I don't want to ride in anything that's his!"

"Well, I'm sorry, but we might not have a choice. We can't dwell on what's happened to us right now and we sure can't walk very far. We've got to find the truck or we can find the car so we can get away from here."

Terry Lynn sobbed and said, "Yeah, you're right and I think I can walk, hopefully long enough to find that awful truck. I just won't think about my frightful experience in that truck." Then she tried to stand up, but she fell back onto the ground. Rae Ann asked her to lay there for a couple of minutes. Hopefully, she could regain some of her strength back. She knew that Terry Lynn needed some food and water.

"I know where some water is," said Rae Ann. I've got to go get you some. I'll be back in a minute."

Terry Lynn spoke while Rae Ann was still deep in thought. She said, "No, you can't leave me here alone, Rae Ann."

"I'll just be a few feet away. I'll be in plain sight, so don't worry. Terry Lynn, you have to drink some water."

Then she left, without giving Terry Lynn another chance to say anything. She was back within a minute or two with some fresh water.

"You have to drink this. You're so dehydrated right now. Please. Just open your mouth, Terry Lynn. I'll help you with the bottle." She gave the water to Terry Lynn very slowly at first, making sure that Terry Lynn didn't have any problems drinking it. Then Terry Lynn swallowed larger amounts until the water was gone.

"My throat is sore, but the water was good. I feel a little bit better. Thanks Rae Ann."

"Where's Willie, Rae Ann? Do you think he's all right? I'm his wife Rae Ann. We got married. That's why he's been away. We're goin' to have a big, beautiful wedding with all of y'all there real soon."

Rae Ann was relieved to hear that Randy might not have kidnapped Willie—at least, she hoped not. Where can he be?

"Willie? I haven't seen Willie, Terry Lynn. Was he with you when you left your house?" asked Rae Ann.

"No. He heard that you could be missing, so he decided to go look for you. He wasn't in my car, but he was up ahead of me until I lost sight of him. He didn't even know that I had left the house. He told me to stay home, but I was worried about him. I didn't want him to be alone, so I followed him. He didn't even know that I was in the car behind him. One minute he was there and I just turned my head for a second. All of a sudden he disappeared. How could that have happened during that second? It was as if he just vanished! The next thing I knew, my car window was smashed to pieces, a fist came right at me, and when I opened my eyes, my head was throbbing and there was a terrible stench. I've never smelled anything that bad in my life.

Rae Ann said, trying to keep from alarming Terry Lynn, "Don't worry and don't panic. We'll find him. He's not at Randy's house. Maybe he decided to get some help. I know it's difficult to relax, but you're losing so much blood and you're shaking so bad, so you've got to try. I don't know how bad off you are, but I know it's serious, and I can tell that you're going to need a lot of medical attention. First we've got to get out of here. Unfortunately, we can't call for help quite yet, because the phone isn't exactly workin'. I must say that the telephone is truly a wonderful invention, especially the phone line. It has so many uses."

"Well, I don't know what you're talking about, Rae Ann, but whatever it is, must be good, and I can hardly wait to hear the whole story." Then Terry Lynn tried to smile, even with her bloody, swollen lips.

"Don't worry Terry Lynn. Everything's goin' to be all right." Then she held Terry Lynn's head and stroked her hair in an attempt to comfort her. "We can barely walk, but we need try to walk as far as we can and we need to hurry or we won't be able to go anywhere. Let's just hold on to each other and get going. We've got to get help, so you can go home soon and make plans for your wedding."

Neither one of them could run, so they just limped and held on to each other and to unruly branches that extended from the trees on both sides of the women and to whatever else they could grab onto to hold themselves up as they walked until the truck or any other vehicle was found that they could possibly drive.

Finally, they saw the truck and Rae Ann said, "You can sit right here for a minute. I'll drive the truck over here for you."

"No Rae Ann! I don't want to be left alone. I don't ever want to be alone again!" Terry Lynn started to cry hysterically.

"All right, Terry Lynn. Don't cry. We'll walk right over there somehow, and I'll help you get into the truck with me." So they slowly walked to the truck and then Rae Ann said confidently, "Now, the next step is for us to get in and see if we can find the key. I think I know where it might be," said Rae Ann. "I wish we could find a cell phone, but we know that ol' coot wouldn't have anything like that around. Terry Lynn, are you okay?"

"I feel cold, Rae Ann."

"Here you are. You can wear my jacket. That's all we have. You know what? I can check to see if we can get the heat goin' in this ol' rig."

"That's fine. Thanks, Rae Ann. Rae Ann? No matter what the outcome is here today, I want you to know that I love you, and your whole family. Y'all have been wonderful to me all these years. Can you tell my family that I love them all, too?"

"Shhh . . . now don't talk. Just try to rest the best way you can, and as much as you can."

Terry Lynn felt a little disoriented and she had difficulty sitting up. "Will this seat lay back?"

"I'm not sure. That's one thing that I never found out."

Rae Ann knew that they both needed a lot of medical attention.

"We need a dern phone! What are we going to do? I'm sick and tired of this!" Rae Ann was furious.

"Terry Lynn, can you think of anything else that we need to do? Well, there's not much gas, but I guess it's enough to get us to a phone or something. After I find the key, we better buckle up 'cause we're in for one hell of a ride. Maybe if we get lucky, the police will see us on the road. We won't have to worry about the gas then, will we Terry Lynn?" There was no sound. Terry Lynn never answered her question. Rae Ann hoped that she just fell asleep for a little while, but she feared the worst. Rae Ann knew that she should hurry. She was glad that she remembered the old days. She knew where Randy used to hide his keys. There should be a string under the seat on the driver's side with the key attached to it. Luckily, Randy kept some of his old habits, even as an adult so when Rae Ann checked, there indeed, was a string and there was the key attached to it. She started up the truck and without hesitance, she sped off.

First, Rae Ann drove down the long stretch of road until she came to the Colson's farm, where she decided to stop and get help.

Rae Ann looked ahead and caught a glimpse of Nell galloping towards the farmhouse. She just hoped that the Colson's still lived there. Unfortunately, they weren't there. There was water and hay outside. Rae Ann decided that once she found help, she would seek help for Nell too.

"Damn! They're not here either. I hope he didn't kill them too. What do we do now? I've got to think. Why on earth can't I think and remember what I need to right now?"

She started to regain more of her memory, but it was still coming back too slowly. She remembered that she was in another car accident, but this time she was in her car by herself and crashed at the riverside. She remembered that there was something strange about it. There was recollection of a car there that looked just like the car that ran her daughters and her off the road at the time of the first accident. Now she believes that Randy 'caused both accidents.

"We're headed for the river, 'cause we can drive there faster than we can drive to town. I believe my car's there, anyway. Even if I can't get it running, my cell phone should be in the glove compartment. We're not losing this battle without a good fight. Do you hear that Terry Lynn? Don't give up. We have to believe that we're going to find help real soon."

Rae Ann hoped that her car was still at the river. It just had to be there because that's where she was headed. She was pretty sure that her cell phone was there too, but hopefully, someone spotted her car and called for help. How could they not see a mangled, bright red 1967 Mustang? Rae Ann had no idea of exactly how long she laid there by the river after the crash, but someone was bound to have seen it by now, unless that conniving Randy had moved it or something. She wasn't about to start worrying about that right now until she knew for sure.

She drove down the old road for nearly two hours, and then finally, she saw Randy's car. Now, she knew that she and Terry Lynn couldn't be far from the river. There was still gas in the truck, so she continued to drive it down the road. Besides, Rae Ann was concerned and felt that it would take too much time to try to put Terry Lynn inside the car. Rae Ann didn't want to jeopardize Terry Lynn's health or her own health.

Rae Ann thought she saw some water a little farther down from the road that they were now on. Rae Ann continued to feel weaker. She wasn't breathing properly, and she was having chest pains, and she ached all over. She didn't want to look at Terry Lynn, because she was afraid of what she might see. She was worried about her condition though and she was very afraid for Terry Lynn, so she decided to forget her own fears, look at Terry Lynn, and to try to help her in any way that she could. So she looked, and felt nauseous when she saw that blood was dripping from Terry Lynn's mouth. There were puddles of blood on the floor of the truck. Rae Ann then felt for a pulse and thankfully, she did find one, so she knew that it was a good sign. Then she listened for a heartbeat and thought that she heard that too. Terry Lynn was breathing faintly, too, so Rae Ann decided that all she could do is to try to find someone to help just as quickly as she could.

Now, she had her cousin Willie on her mind. She knew Willie should be with Terry Lynn—especially now. Rae Ann wondered if Randy had gotten her cousin, and if Willie's still alive. She still hadn't caught sight of him and she didn't know where to start looking, but she knew that she had no time to search for him right now. Rae Ann knew in her heart that Terry Lynn's and her time might be coming to an end very soon, so she had to put every single second that they had to good use.

Rae Ann stepped on the gas pedal, exceeding the speed limit until she reached the river. The gas tank was near empty, but it didn't matter because Rae Ann couldn't drive any farther anyway.

She managed to open the door on her side of the truck and practically fell out head first and then she just dragged her limp, almost lifeless body through the grass, the dirt, and the mud, pulling herself with her arms and her hands until she reached the water. She was so thirsty, but she didn't make an attempt to drink the river water. She had no more strength to move herself any farther. The water looked so calm, so peaceful, and tranquil to her. The sun shone down on the water, making reflections of beautiful, transparent colors that glistened with the rippling current. She loved the land that she grew up in. Virginia was always her home, and it had all she ever needed. She felt it was a beautiful land, and that there was never a need to live anywhere else.

She didn't see her Mustang in sight, but she was convinced that she was close to the area where the terrible living nightmare began.

Rae Ann wasn't quite sure if anyone would find Terry Lynn or her in time. Undoubtedly, they could die at any moment now without anyone even knowing. Rae Ann made peace with herself and softly said "Grandma . . . Granddaddy, am I coming home today? Will I be back with y'all again?" This is what Rae Ann wondered as she tilted her head back, lifting it just above the ground. Then she moved her head upward and looked up to the sky with her sore, tired, squinted eyes.

CHAPTER 21

During that time, Willie was still in the hole in the ground. It turned out to be some sort of man-made grave. Willie wondered if Randy had dug it up. He didn't realize that Randy had dug the hole to bury him and Terry Lynn in.

It felt like eternity, but finally, he heard voices and thank goodness, it wasn't Randy's voice. He could hear something that sounded like some sort of walkie—talkie. Willie was so happy and so relieved to hear the voices and the sounds of possibly a police radio. He started calling out once again, as loud as he could.

Willie shouted, "Hey! I'm down here!

Someone then asked, "Are you Willie—Russ's son?"

"Yeah, I'm Willie. You're Sheriff Jenkins aren't you?"

"Yes, I am. I've known your family ever since you were a baby."

"Yeah, I remember you Officer Jenkins. You took us all down to the police station when Mary Beth and Sammy disappeared and our cousin Lori was murdered."

"That's right buddy. Now I'm here to try to help you and your family again."

Are you having any trouble breathing? If you're not, then keep talking and we'll try to follow the sound of your voice so we can find you."

"I'm breathing just fine, but it's cold and dark down here. It's a big hole and the sides are slippery and unlevelled. Did somebody dig this hole?"

"Yes, we believe so."

"Is somebody tryin' to catch something in this hole?"

"Yeah buddy, you can bet on that."

"Okay, buddy, we're going to get some rope, so we can pull you out of there just as fast as we can. How does that sound?"

"It sounds great."

"We know, Willie boy." We can hardly wait either. We're glad we found you alive. By the way, you're speaking to Officer Jacobs now. I've known your family for years, too."

"Yeah, I remember you too, Officer Jacobs."

"Okay, now we're going to toss the rope to you. You need to fling it over your head and make a lasso, so get ready, once it's wrapped around your waist, you can tighten it and let us know when you're ready to come up."

"I've got it. There now, it's wrapped tight around my waist, so now, I reckon I'm ready." Willie could hardly wait to get out of that uninhabitable hole in the ground.

"All right fellas . . . one . . . . two . . . three! PULL!" said Officer Jenkins. So they pulled Willie back up to the surface. Officer Jenkins knew that the hole that Willie was in was a grave. It didn't appear that the work had been finished, so Officer Jenkins knew that this was a definite clue to the whereabouts of a killer-possibly of the killer they had been looking for all these years. It also meant that the killer would probably be back to finish digging the grave. Officer Jenkins didn't want to tell Willie about his suspicions because he didn't want Willie to panic or to try to handle the situation on his own. He asked one of the deputies to take Willie to one of the cars to sit and rest for a minute and then go ahead and question him about the events that led up to Willie falling into the grave. He didn't want them to tell Willie that it was definitely a grave though, so there was no mention about it by the other officers.

Once Willie was taken far enough away from them, Officer Jenkins said to the other officers and to the detective, "I think we've got something here. We might need to call for backup. We'll need to call the FBI too. We might finally have a big break in this case."

After questioning Willie, they knew that Randy had abducted Willie and that he probably was a killer, too. Willie told them that Rae Ann hadn't been seen and about Aaron, Heather, and Trisha searching for her. He then used Officer Jacobs mobile phone to call home. He longed to hear Terry Lynn's voice, and he knew she'd be relieved to know that he was with the police and the sheriff's department. Well, Willie dialed the telephone number, but there was no answer. He told Officer Jacobs and Officer Jenkins that Terry Lynn was supposed to stay home, so she should be there. Willie called home, Charles and his family's home, Terry Lynn's parent's home, and everyone else he could think of only to find out that she hadn't visited anyone, or called any of them either. Then the officers suspected that Terry Lynn could be in extreme danger, but they didn't want to alarm Willie with their suspicions until they had some proof. Willie was lucky to break away from Randy and they hoped that Terry Lynn was that lucky too, if Randy had kidnapped her.

Willie told them that Randy had kept him tied up in his car for a few days after driving to some remote area that Willie rarely ever went to. As a matter of fact, Willie hadn't gone back to that area since he first learned about the people who ended up missing after being in that part of the woods. The stories about the *Dirt Man* and the memories all came back. Willie was still haunted by these memories, just as everyone else was. He paused for a minute or two, still feeling some of the fear of the past and then he once again focused on the present and continued to tell the grim details of how Randy forced Willie inside Randy's car until he pushed Willie out of the car into some dirt near some old building that Willie didn't recognize. Willie was then pushed inside the building, and Randy untied his hands. Randy left, and locked the door from the outside of the building. It took Willie almost a week to figure out how to get out of there and once he did get away, he started to run back towards his home, but then Randy caught up with him. Willie told the police about the fight between them and how he ended up in the hole.

"So Randy's still out there, running around loose Willie? You know, we better check his home. Do you think he'd go back to where he grew up?"

"I believe so, and I know a good shortcut to the house," said Willie. "I can probably show you better than I can tell you."

"Well, I think we better get you some medical attention at the hospital first buddy. The ambulance will be here in a moment or two."

"You have a knot on your head about the size of a golf ball. Listen, we want to make sure you're all right. Then you can help us. I think your wife wants you in *mint condition* when she sees you. Don't you Willie?"

"I don't want to go to a hospital yet. I'd rather ride with you. I'll go to a hospital a little later. Listen, my health is fine right now."

Just then they got a call from the FBI, who had already made progress. Then Officer Jenkins said to Willie, "Well buddy, we're going to let you have your way. We're going to let you ride with us to the river.

Officer Jacobs said, "Y'all take Willie to one of our cars, and then come back over here so Officer Jenkins and I can have a word with y'all about a new break in this case."

Willie looked with curiosity at one officer and then at the other, trying to read their faces and then said, "Okay, what is it that you're not saying? Don't you think that I have a right to know about any new facts concerning my relatives?"

"Willie, we don't know all the facts ourselves yet. We'll let you know just as soon as we possibly can."

"Well, all right then, I guess one of you better hurry up and walk me to one of your cars so you can start talkin' and I can start finding out what I need to know."

Officer Jacobs nodded his head in agreement with Willie. As soon as Willie was taken to one of the police cars, Officer Jacobs told the other officers that he had just received word that Rae Ann and Terry Lynn had been found and that they were *hanging on for dear life*. Terry Lynn was found in Randy's old truck and Rae Ann was found by the riverside, partially in the shallow water. The FBI had quickly located Aaron, Heather, and Trisha and flew them by helicopter to the river.

Officer Jacobs then said, "The ambulances are on the way to the river. I hope we all make it there in time. Willie will be taken with his wife to the nearest hospital. Now, let's get going and I mean fast! We don't have a moment to waste!"

The sirens were turned on and the police drove at high speeds to the river. The roads were almost free of traffic at that time of the day, so they were able to get there quickly.

Willie, still feeling curious and worried, asked "Okay, let me ask you again-what's going on? Can't you tell me anything? Why are the sirens on? We're not headed towards Randy's family's house. Before anything else could be said, he recognized the area they were in and said, we're goin' towards the river aren't we?"

"That's right Mr. Matthews, we are driving to the river and you'll be fully aware and fully informed of everything we can tell you just as soon as we get there," replied one of the younger officers. Willie never met this particular officer before.

"That's a relief. Then things can get taken care of and get back to normal again. I'm a newlywed and I know I'm going to be in trouble with my wife already when I get back home. I'll have some serious explaining to do."

The young officer wished that things could be that easily taken care of. He wished he could express the sorrow he felt for Willie and Willie's new wife, but he followed procedures, knowing why it was so important to do so.

"Mr. Matthews? We'll be there in just a few short minutes."

"Well, you're sure making me feel important and old too. I appreciate the respect and your courtesy, but now you're part of our Caroline family out here in the country, and you're a new friend of mine too because you're helping my family. Just call me Willie like everybody else does. Then he smiled.

The policeman looked through his rear-view mirror and winked and nodded and answered "Yes sir, I mean okay Willie, and thanks. Outside of the job, my first name is William too, but I'm called Bill and sometimes Billy and my last name is Maynard and my partner here is Officer Townshend."

Then the Officer William (Bill) Maynard looked at his partner who was sitting quietly in the front seat with him on the passenger's side. The other officer jumped into the conversation at that point and told Willie that his first name is Roger.

The two policemen knew that Rae Ann's brother and sister would undoubtedly go to the river and most, if not all, of the other cousins, brothers, sisters, aunts, uncles, and grandparents would be there too, along with friends, unless they go straight to the hospital.

We're almost there. We just need to go about one-quarter mile down the road now.

Willie looked through the window and in the distance; he could see ambulances, police cars, and officials in unmarked cars, helicopters, and fire trucks. There he sat, still calm until he saw Aaron with his medical bag. He leaned forward, feeling very concerned, and shouted, "Oh, no! My wife! My wife! She's on a stretcher! What happened to her? Stop this damn car! Stop now! Please! You've got to stop!"

The car stopped and he jumped out, and ran to his wife as she was taken on the stretcher into the ambulance. Before the doors of the ambulance were shut, Willie told Officer Jacobs to let the others know that he'd see them at the hospital. The sirens were turned on and the ambulance left with Willie and Terry Lynn inside, as they headed to the hospital. Inside the ambulance, Willie was by Terry Lynn's side and he leaned downward next to her head and whispered softly in her ear, "We're going to have our big wedding just as soon as you get out of the hospital honey; just as soon as you're well enough. It'll be the most beautiful wedding in the world—just like you wanted. I love you Terry Lynn. I can't lose you." Then he sobbed.

Terry Lynn's parents drove their car to the hospital. Some of Willie and Terry Lynn's friends followed her parents there too, unknowing of what was to happen to their dear friends. They'd known Terry Lynn all their lives and became friends with Willie many years ago.

Barely conscious and frail, Rae Anne could hear the faint sounds of voices surrounding her. The familiar voices were Heather's and Trish's. Rae Ann could feel their tears trickling down on her face and she could hear Heather crying and saying, "Mama, we know. Mama! I said we know. We found copies of your medical records in your house. We're not going to let you die. Hang on, mama. You've got to take medicine now. It's prednisone that just might help save your life. You'll have to take other drugs, too. Mama, you have to stay with us because we all love you. You just can't let go. We all need you in our lives. Uncle Ray and Aunt Sue and everybody else is here including Uncle Willie. I know that makes you happy. He's hurt, but he'll be okay. He's in the ambulance with Terry Lynn. You'll see him at the hospital. Just then, Rae Ann heard a whisper saying, "Rae Ann, it's me. It's your mama. Be strong."

"Aaron said Terry Lynn lost a significant amount of blood, but that everything in their power will be done for her. Mama, we have to believe that all of y'all will pull through without any complications. Be strong, just as your grandma and granddaddy taught you."

Terry Lynn and Willie left in the ambulance which left for the hospital.

Just after that was all said, Aaron walked over to Rae Ann and knelt down beside her. He had his medical bag with him. He got a syringe out and filled it with the drug that was recently approved for her disease. Rae Ann had previously signed the necessary forms which gave Aaron the authority to legally administer the drug to Rae Ann. This was done just a few short months ago. She had signed the form, but at that time, she was reluctant to do so. She struggled with herself emotionally about it, but finally reasoned with herself and decided that if there was any hope for her to live a normal life in the future; she'd sign as she was expected to do—but not without reminding Aaron that he was still obligated by law, to keep everything concerning her health, completely confidential. Rae Ann didn't know that Aaron was no longer her primary doctor.

Although, Heather felt Aaron was still the best doctor for her mother, and wasn't totally convinced that her mother should have a different doctor, she accepted his decision to discontinue as Rae Ann's physician. She knew he gave very serious consideration to the matter. She stood by Aaron in every decision he made.

Within minutes, the medics put Rae Ann on a stretcher and whisked her away into the ambulance, but not without Rae Ann first hearing Aaron commenting that if the drug worked, it could mean that Rae Ann's life would have a new beginning with lots of love and happiness that she so desperately wanted.

Once Rae Ann heard this, her vital signs almost magically stabilized and she was free of pain, so probably emotionally, she was better, too. The medication started to take effect. There was a medic inside the ambulance, but he was unaware of how much she could comprehend. They didn't believe that she would react to this drug in the same way that she would to the other drugs that were given to her for her illness. The drug actually took effect more slowly in comparison to the other drugs.

A couple of minutes later, she overheard the sheriff and some of the other officers talking. They were standing just outside the ambulance. She could still comprehend what was being said although she was starting to feel a little woozy and sleepy. The sheriff said, "Well, we've finally caught the son-of-a-bitch that's responsible for some of the killing of our town folks. We just didn't have enough proof that Randy was the one who'd been committing all these kidnappings and murders all these years. Although, we have all the proof that we need now, we all know that he has some family members around and we haven't seen any of them for quite some time, so if they're involved in any of this in any way, then it's still going to be a while before our communities are safe because they're still on the loose and it might not be the end of the killings yet. We know that Randy's guilty of some of the murders, but he isn't guilty of the first murders that were committed more than 20 years ago. Maybe, his daddy is, though. Randy was only two or three years old when the killing spree first started."

The sheriff walked away from the ambulance, pointed his finger abruptly in the air, and exclaimed angrily, "If they are involved, and they're still alive, we'll find them. It's just going to take a little more time. Once all the evidence is collected and processed, we'll know who's guilty and who's not. There's plenty of proof now. Finally, we'll all be able to put all our fears aside for good."

"Oh, by the way, let me remind you all, that no one, and I mean absolutely no one can even attempt to question Rae Ann, Terry Lynn, or Willie at this time, and not until the doctors give their approval."

Rae Ann began to feel frightened, and started to tremble at the thought of more kidnappings and murders. She was sickened from the thought of herself falling prey again, and to have to relive the horror all over again. This was just too unbearable for her, and suddenly, she screamed, and screamed again hysterically, until she made no sound at all. There wasn't even the slightest movement. The medics jumped into the ambulance, put the siren on and sped off to the hospital.

The sheriff, the other officers, and everyone else there, were torn with sadness. This was one of the most traumatic and horrific cases they'd ever had. They genuinely cared for all of their town's people. Hopefully, no one would ever encounter anything like this ever again. They hoped that Rae Ann would have a full recovery. Ordinarily, the medication wouldn't have taken so long to take full effect on a person. She should have already been asleep or at least relaxed. Aaron assured them that they weren't at fault and told them that because of her ordeal and her physical condition, the medication didn't react the same way. It may have been an adverse effect. She will have to heal physically, deal with her emotions once again, and try to live her life the best way that she knows how.

EPILOGUE . . .

Hopefully, Rae Ann, Terry Lynn, and Willie will be all right and the killings will finally come to an end. What will become of these beautiful, but mysterious country roads now? What will become of Rae Ann's and her loved ones' lives? One can only wonder what the future has in store for them. Will our country areas be as wonderful, as beautiful, as inviting, and as enjoyable as they have so often been through the years? Only time will tell. Let's all find our inner strength just as Rae Ann did until the time comes for us to find out what's in store for us in our own lives. Will the land will be clean and safe from harm as Willie hoped? Will the music keep on playing like a beautiful melodic song in our minds as in Rae Ann's mind? Again, only time will tell. Would you want to go back on those old dirt roads in the country in the dead of night? Will our hopes and our dreams come true and will our lives be fulfilled and will we all really be able to live the lives that we want to live? Do you believe that any of the town folks have gone back there? Did Rae Ann, Willie, Terry Lynn, and any of others that were lucky enough to survive their terrible ordeal, finally have normal lives, or could they be in for mountain slides of treacherous turmoil? Do you believe that it's all finally over? Or, do you think that they might have to endure another horrific experience in those deep, dark wooded areas?

Floatin', goin' . . .

Floatin' on down the river.

Downstream, upstream . . .

The water sure makes me quiver.

Leavin', goin' . . .

I might go on forever.

See me, hear me . . .

The ferocious waves are tryin' to pierce my soul,

As I'm tossed against these rocks.

The timeless river's got a hold on me,

But in the end—I decide what will be.

This ol' endless river's going to set me free.

See me, hear me—know that . . .

One day we'll be together.

I look up high at the big blue sky . . .

It takes my blues away.

Come embrace me now, my kindred soul.

Will you take me now—this way?

Come grace me now

With your love so deep.

Please hear me when I cry.

See me, hear me . . .

'cause I might be coming home today.